LIBBY
ON
WEDNESDAY

Libby on Wednesday

ZILPHA KEATLEY SNYDER

**Delacorte
Press**

Published by
Delacorte Press
Bantam Doubleday Dell Publishing Group, Inc.
666 Fifth Avenue
New York, New York 10103

Library of Congress Cataloging in Publication Data

Snyder, Zilpha Keatley.
    Libby on Wednesday / by Zilpha Keatley Snyder.
        p.cm.
    Summary: Having been put ahead in an accelerated
    eighth grade program by her bizarre and creative family,
    precocious eleven-year-old Libby hates her "socialization"
    process, until she makes some highly original
    friends in a writing workshop.
    ISBN 0-385-29979-6
    [1. Authorship—Fiction.   2. Friendship—Fiction.
    3. Schools—Fiction.]
    I. Title.   PZ7.S68522Li   1990   [Fic]—dc20
            89-34959   CIP   AC

Book design by Andrew Roberts

Manufactured in the United States of America

March 1990

10   9   8   7   6   5   4   3   2   1

BG

To all of you
who said,
"I write too."

LIBBY
ON
WEDNESDAY

"I've decided to quit school again," Libby said.

That did it. All around the table voices hushed in mid-sentence. Shocked alarm quivered in the silence. Even Gillian's cats, the three great Persian puffballs and one sleek Abyssinian, looked up nervously from their favorite spot near the swinging double doors that led into the kitchen. Libby realized at once that she'd made a mistake.

It would have been better, she knew, to have approached the subject more gradually. To have prepared all four of them a little for what was coming, perhaps by giving them some reason for her sudden decision. Not the real one, of course. To tell them the truth about why she had to quit school was out of the question. But she could have mentioned some reasons—and there were many that she could think of—that they might understand and appreciate.

She had, in fact, tried that approach. She had made a stab at preparing Christopher, her father, when she had gone out to the gazebo where he had been working on his poetry to tell him that dinner was ready. Leaning against his desk as he gathered up his pens and notebooks, she had mentioned casually that no one at Morrison Middle School seemed to know anything at all about Socrates. But to her surprise he hadn't seemed shocked or even very much concerned. The calm smile on his thin, deep-eyed face didn't even waver as he patted in the general direction of her cheek and murmured, "Mmm, that is too bad, isn't it."

She was about to say something more on the subject, when Christopher suddenly sat back down, scratched out a line of poetry, and began to scribble rapidly. Realizing that it was a bad time—Christopher was always a little vague and distant when he was working—she had gone looking for someone else.

But the results were much the same in the Great Hall, where she found Gillian, her grandmother, and her grandmother's sister, Cordelia. Although neither of them was writing poetry, they were every bit as preoccupied as Christopher had been. Gillian and Cordelia were arguing, or as they liked to put it, "having a serious discussion." At the moment the discussion seemed to be about politics—one of many subjects on which the two sisters always disagreed. But even though it was an old argument, they seemed to be too busy making the same old points to take much interest in what Libby was trying to tell them about Socrates at Morrison Middle School.

Telling herself she just hadn't gotten their attention, she'd tried a slightly more straightforward approach as soon as they were all seated at the huge old table in the dining room. While the food was being passed around—Elliott's special pot-roasted chicken with lots of fresh vegetables—she'd made her plans carefully. Perched, as she always was

2

at mealtime, on a couple of encyclopedias, since at age eleven she was still too small for the massive McCall House dining room furniture, she'd waited for what seemed a good moment to announce loudly that her eighth-grade math class was currently studying material she'd learned when she was nine years old.

But Elliott had been busy telling Christopher about an attempted theft at the bookstore, and Gillian and Cordelia were still going on about politics. And all four of them seemed as unconcerned about the mathematics she wasn't learning as they had been about Socrates.

Libby was beginning to lose her temper. Usually they were only too interested in everything she had to say as well as everything she had been doing or even thinking, particularly anything about her experiences at Morrison Middle School. And even more particularly anything she really didn't want to talk about. But when she really needed them to listen . . .

Deciding it was necessary to do something drastic, she blurted out her announcement about quitting school—and suddenly had their complete attention.

As the silence lengthened and stiffened, all four of them seemed to lengthen and stiffen too. Sitting around the long oak table, their suddenly erect bodies framed by the ornately carved backs of the huge old chairs, they looked like so many portraits. Like the stiff, solemn portraits with staring eyes that hang on the walls of ancient castles. Particularly Christopher with his poet's face, fine-lined and melancholy, and Gillian in her bright fringed shawl and dangling earrings. For just a fraction of a second Libby's awful load of misery was lightened by an urge to giggle.

3

It was Libby's father—Christopher McCall—who spoke first. Putting down his fork and fishing in his lap for his napkin, he wiped his mustache carefully and said, "What is it, Libby? Is there a problem at school?"

She shrugged. "Not a problem, exactly. I've just been concerned lately that I'm not learning nearly as much as I was before I started school. Why couldn't we just go on the way we were?"

"Ah," Gillian sighed, her worried frown drifting off into soft-eyed daydream. *The Way We Were.* One of my favorite movies. With Robert Redford, you know." She glanced at Cordelia, and her blue eyes, always surprisingly young and lively-looking in her small wrinkled face, went suddenly needle sharp. "Such a handsome man, Redford," she said meaningfully. The meaning was that Robert Redford was better-looking than Charlton Heston—another favorite disagreement between Gillian and her sister.

Gillian McCall, Libby's grandmother, who was always just Gillian—not ever Mrs. McCall and absolutely not Grandma—flipped her fringes over her shoulder dramatically and sighed again before she went on. "Such a beautiful story. And in some ways quite like Graham's and mine."

Everybody smiled. They'd all heard it before—many times. Any conversation about movies, past or present, was sure to start Gillian off about the two main characters in *The Way We Were,* the talented writer and his madcap wife, and how they were so similar to Graham and Gillian McCall. But this time Libby wasn't going to let Gillian's romantic memories change the subject. The subject was that she, Libby McCall, wanted to go back to "the way we were"

4

until last fall—when she'd begun to attend school for the first time, at the rather advanced age of eleven years.

"I've just been thinking about it lately and I've decided I'd really prefer to go back to studying at home." She smiled at each of them, her father first, and her grandmother, and then Elliott and Cordelia. "Unless it would be too much trouble for everybody. To start teaching me again, I mean."

She knew what they would say. "Darling!" they said, and "Libby dearest, don't be ridiculous." It was hard to tell exactly who was saying what. With their sentences overlapping as if they were singing a round, they chanted soothing phrases, solo and duet. Phrases such as, "You weren't any trouble. You know we all loved being your teachers. We all loved being the Libby McCall Private Academy. Didn't we, Elliott? Didn't we, Cordelia? Of course we did."

The Libby McCall Private Academy had started after Libby's first day in kindergarten, when she'd come home and announced that she wasn't going back. She couldn't remember exactly why she'd come to that decision so quickly, except that it had something to do with the fact that there wasn't any good reading material in the classroom.

No one had made any fuss about it then. Everyone had agreed that there really wasn't much point in making a person who could already read *The New York Times* spend the better part of a year learning the alphabet. And since Elliott had once taught school and still had a teacher's credential, the school authorities hadn't objected either. Dropping out of kindergarten had been very simple and easy, and it seemed to Libby that dropping out of a seventh- and eighth-grade combination shouldn't be any more difficult.

"Well, then," Libby said, trying to sound as if it were all settled, "let's do it again." Choosing her grandmother as the one most apt to be on her side, she smiled, tucking in the corners of her mouth to emphasize her dimples—dimples that were especially admired by Gillian, from whom they were so obviously inherited. "The way we were. All right, Gilly?"

But it seemed it wasn't going to be quite that easy. As the four of them looked around, checking each other's faces, they all began to frown again. Libby sighed. It was so like them, taking forever to make a decision, except of course when Mercedes was at home. But Mercedes O'Brien, Libby's absentee mother, wasn't at home and probably wouldn't be for several months. And this couldn't wait that long. It couldn't, in fact, wait even one more week. "Well?" she asked finally.

"Well," Christopher said, "I don't know. We promised your mother, you know. We promised that you'd attend public school. And you've been doing so well."

Libby winced. She'd been afraid they'd say something like that. That someone would mention what a fine social adjustment she'd been making and how right her mother had been to insist that learning to get along with your peers was an important part of education.

"I know," she said. "It was all Mercedes' idea." She tried to make her smile say that she was mature enough to be amused at her mother's strange theories—theories that might be popular and perhaps even useful in New York City but had nothing to do with the life of Libby McCall of

Morrison, California. "I know," she said again. "Because I needed to be socialized. Well, what I think is six months is long enough to socialize anyone, especially a person who is a fast learner. You've always said I was a fast learner. What I think is that I've finished the course. I'm as socialized as I'm ever going to be—at least by Morrison Middle School."

"Libby, I'm getting an impression that . . ." On the other side of the table Elliott was leaning forward, his long, narrow face crinkling with concern, and his sloping, exclamation-mark eyebrows quivering the way they always did when he was worried. He studied her thoughtfully for a moment as if he were trying to read her mind and then went on. "I'm getting a strong impression that . . ." He paused again, sniffed the air like a bird dog, and suddenly dashed from the room.

As Elliott rushed toward the kitchen door, he startled the cats, who stopped in mid-lick and scattered—Goliath under Gillian's chair; Salome and Isadora under the sideboard; and Ariel, as usual, straight up. Racing up the heavy old velvet draperies, already frazzled by frequent high-speed escapes from many other real or pretend dangers, she peered over the edge of the valance with her astonishing Abyssinian eyes. Everyone except Cordelia laughed. Elliott, who also worried about such things as the frazzling of draperies, might not have either, but he was in the kitchen, so the laughter was almost unanimous.

For a moment Libby felt better than she had since early that morning, but the heavy weight of gloom returned quickly. The others' smiles faded quickly, too, and Christopher, Gillian, and Cordelia went back to worried frowns and expectant glances at the kitchen door. They were obviously counting on Elliott to solve the problem in the kitchen and come back and solve Libby's, whatever it might be.

For almost as long as Libby could remember, everyone had counted on Elliott Garner to take care of problems that shouldn't really have been his responsibility. Elliott's only real responsibility should have been managing his bookstore, but here in the McCall House, as people called it—the shabby, rundown, silly old McCall mansion—he'd somehow gotten stuck with managing the kitchen and laundry and Christopher's bank account, and just about everything else one might mention.

Christopher called Elliott his agent and manager, and Gillian called him an angel sent from heaven to save the McCalls from bankruptcy, squalor, and chronic indigestion. Cordelia, of course, wasn't quite as enthusiastic about Elliott, but then Cordelia made it a point never to be enthusiastic about the same things as her sister. What she called Elliott was "The Man Who Came to Dinner," which meant, of course, that he'd come on a visit and forgotten to leave. Of course Cordelia was a fine one to talk, since she'd done pretty much the same thing, but then she was a relative, and that, according to Cordelia, entitled her to make long-term —or even permanent—visits.

Now they were obviously counting on Elliott to find out why Libby suddenly wanted to quit school. He'd solved so many of her previous problems. He was, for one thing, a marvelous math and science teacher, subjects for which no one else in the family had any particular aptitude. And for another, he was a talented builder and repairman.

Over the years he had repaired any number of things of importance to Libby, delicate old things mostly, from her grandfather's collections—such as music boxes, cuckoo clocks, and all kinds of fragile antique toys. Not to mention the most important of all—the Treehouse, the incredible, incomparable Treehouse that had once been Christopher's but now was the private and exclusive property of Libby herself.

Over the years it had been Elliott's repair work that had kept the Treehouse safe and sound and usable, and Libby would always be grateful to him for that. But not even Elliott would be able to repair the damage that had been done at Morrison Middle School—even though the rest of the family was obviously expecting him to try.

"Libby dear," Elliott began again when he finally returned to the table with a bowl of slightly scorched gravy and Gillian's cats had crept out from under chairs and tables. "I have the feeling something must have gone wrong at school today. Was it something about the visiting author? Did it have something to do with meeting Arnold Axminster?"

Libby looked up quickly. It had been at least a month since she'd told them that Arnold Axminster, one of her favorite authors, was going to be visiting Morrison Middle School. She'd only mentioned it once, briefly, and since that time she deliberately hadn't said anything more. Leave it to Elliott to remember.

Until that moment she hadn't meant to tell them everything. Or anything, really. She'd counted on their letting her quit school simply because, as far as they knew, there wasn't any good reason not to. Because she had been sent to public school for a particular purpose, and as far as they knew that purpose had been achieved. But now Elliott's unexpected question suggested a new possibility—a way of convincing them without actually giving away the whole truth.

"Yes, you guessed it, Elliott. Something terrible happened today, and it was all Arnold Axminster's fault."

They stared at her, at each other, and back again, their eyes saying, "How dreadful. How shocking. Whatever can it mean? What can it mean, Elliott?"

It was Cordelia who spoke first. "Whatever do you mean, Libby?"

Libby made her face into a tragic mask, banishing the dimples and pulling down the corners of her mouth. "I mean," she said, "that Mr. Arnold Axminster, the famous writer, visited Morrison Middle School today and did something that will probably ruin my entire future existence."

She paused and checked the effect. Christopher and Elliott looked bewildered and worried. Gillian, who couldn't help loving a good tragedy, even her own granddaughter's, looked mostly excited. And Cordelia looked scandalized. Cordelia was easy to scandalize.

Libby allowed herself a sad little smile—sad but hopeful. "My entire future," she repeated, "ruined! Unless, of course, I'm allowed to quit school."

"It's really ironic," she told them. *(Ironic,* a word she no longer used at school, had long been a favorite at home.) "I was *so* excited when I heard that he was coming —that Arnold Axminster was actually coming to Morrison Middle School in person. You know how many of his books I've read, and when I found out I was going to get to see him in person, I was really thrilled. And then he goes and ruins my life. Don't you think that's ironic?"

"Yes," everybody said. "Yes, yes. Ironic. But what happened? What exactly happened, Libby?" They were all listening carefully now. All four of them had pushed aside their plates and were leaning forward across the table.

Libby considered for a moment. How much could she tell without including the part that would give everything away? Tucking her hair behind her ears with both hands, she took a deep breath and began. "It all happened because of the Literary Festival. I didn't tell you about the Literary Festival because—well, just because. But anyway, that was why Arnold Axminster was asked to come to the school."

"Libby!" Cordelia broke in. "What happened? Don't drag it out so. What did that man do? Tell us!"

"AUNT Cordelia," Libby said, which was an ironical way of pointing out that nobody else in the McCall household cared about titles. Certainly Christopher never insisted on being called Father, and Gillian said that *grandmother* was a generic label instead of an individual's name and she preferred to be an individual. But Cordelia thought titles were important, so Libby called her AUNT, or even GREAT-AUNT, when she was being particularly Cordelia-ish. *"AUNT* Cordelia," she said again. "I *am* telling you. I didn't want to tell anybody, but if I must go into it, I have to tell it right—the way it all happened."

"Leave the child alone, Cordelia," Gillian said. "She's a McCall, and she has to tell a story in the proper order. It's in her blood."

"So," Libby went on, "the other part of the Literary Festival was the writing contest and—"

"A writing contest?" they said. "Why didn't you tell us? Did you enter something? You won, didn't you? You must have won."

She knew that would be their reaction—the family would take it for granted that the granddaughter of Graham and the daughter of Christopher McCall would write a hundred times better than anyone else at Morrison Middle School. She waited patiently for the uproar to die down. *"That,"* she told them, "is exactly why I didn't tell you. You would have insisted that I enter one of my stories, and I didn't want to. At least I didn't want to at first. Well, actually I never wanted to, but Ms. Ostrowski kept after me and after me until I finally said I would. So at the last minute I entered a chapter of *Rainbow in the Dust.*"

"I quite understand," Elliott said. "I understand why you didn't want to tell us. I suppose that you were afraid that you might not win and that we might be disappointed. I imagine that—"

"No," Libby interrupted. "That wasn't it. What I was afraid of was that I *might* win." She looked at her father.

Christopher was nodding. Libby watched him as she went on. Her father was an extremely private person and a poet besides. If anyone could understand how she felt, it would be he. "I might win, and if I did, I might have to get up on the stage in front of everyone, and maybe I'd even have to read some of my story out loud and . . ." Christopher shuddered. Libby had known he would understand.

"You see how it was?" she said. "But then Ms. Ostrowski kept asking me, and finally I decided I would enter something. What I was thinking was that if I did win, I could always pretend I was sick on the day of the festival so I wouldn't have to do all the . . ." She shrugged. "You know. All the ribbons and prizes and . . ." A grin oozed out through her tragic mask. Jumping up onto her chair, she bowed grandly to right and left. "Thank you, thank you, ladies and gentlemen and boys and girls, for this great honor. I don't know why I'm thanking you because you didn't have anything to do with it, and you probably hate me because I won a prize and you didn't, but winners are always supposed to get up in front of everybody and say stupid things, so thanks again, and—help! Let me out of here!" Making a terror-stricken face, she bowed again hastily, jumped down, and dashed toward the door.

They all laughed and they were still smiling when Libby came back to her chair. For a moment she smiled back—ruefully. A rueful smile was the best she could do under the circumstances. Their laughter certainly didn't change anything. She'd always acted things out for them—a tendency she'd no doubt inherited from her actress mother—and they were always an enthusiastic audience. But at the moment even a standing ovation on their part wouldn't have made her feel much better.

"So," she said, "that was that! Except for deciding whether to have food poisoning or just a terrible headache on the big day. But then, when I hadn't heard anything by yesterday, I asked Ms. Ostrowski and she said she wasn't on the judging committee but she'd heard that the winners had been chosen and notified already. So I was sure I hadn't won. And so, since I really did want to see what Arnold Axminster looked like, I decided not to be sick today after all and—"

"What did he look like?" Gillian asked.

"Look like?" Libby had to think for a moment. "Tall. Tall, with a wide face and shaggy eyebrows. And lots of wavy white hair."

"Umm," Gillian nodded approvingly. "A handsome man. Writers are always beautiful men."

"And he gave a talk during assembly," Libby went on, "a talk about writing and his books, and then Mr. Shoemaker asked him to read the names of the winners of the writers' contest, and I was sure it would be all right because I thought all the winners had been notified. And then . . ." Libby paused dramatically and they all leaned forward.

14

"And then Arnold Axminster read, 'First prize—*Rainbow in the Dust,* by Elizabeth McCall.' "

Gillian and Elliott looked delighted, and Christopher smiled cautiously, holding back until he knew how it all turned out. But Cordelia was angry. "Well," she said, "Elizabeth Portia McCall, you should be ashamed of yourself, worrying us all for no reason." She lifted her chin high and began rearranging her hairdo, pulling pins out of the long braids coiled at the back of her neck and stabbing them back in fiercely. "You're telling us that your life was ruined by having to stand up in front of your classmates to accept a prize. Just another example of McCall artistic temperament, I suppose. Well, what I think is—"

"No, Aunt Cordelia, that isn't it at all," Libby said. "In fact, that part of it, in the assembly, really wasn't so bad after all. All I had to do was walk up on stage and shake Arnold Axminster's hand and accept a certificate. I didn't have to say anything, and no one read any of the winning stories or anything embarrassing like that. But then Mr. Shoemaker announced that as part of their prize all the winners were going to have a private meeting with Mr. Axminster, to talk about writing and get his advice on their writing careers."

Cordelia stopped stabbing her hairdo and leaned forward. "A private meeting!" she said. "I knew it. What did that man do?"

"*No!* Aunt Cordelia. It wasn't anything like that. All of the prizewinners together met with Arnold Axminster in the reading lab, and Ms. Ostrowski was there, too."

Cordelia relaxed, and watching her, Libby had to smile —an *ironic,* inward smile. Of course Cordelia *would* think that made it all right. That having a meeting with all the other winners made everything just wonderful. "There were five winners," she said. "A first and second and third and two honorable mentions." She winced, remembering. Remembering particularly the honorable mentions.

They were all staring at her, confused and worried, not understanding at all. Libby sighed. "One of the winners was a boy named Gary Greene," she blurted out stupidly. Stupid because the name Gary Greene meant nothing to them. She'd never mentioned him before. She hadn't ever told them anything about him and she wasn't about to now.

"Gary Greene?" Christopher asked, his puzzled frown saying that he sensed that the name had some special meaning.

Libby shrugged in what she hoped was an offhand manner. "He's in my homeroom. He's—well, he's someone I know. I'd seen the others but I really didn't know them. There was a girl named Wendy or something like that. And then there was a very large girl with pink hair."

"Pink?" they all said in perfect unison.

Libby grinned, and Gillian laughed out loud. "I know, dear," she said. "Sometimes we sound like a Greek chorus. But pink? Really?"

"Yes, really. But not naturally, of course," Libby said. "It's dyed pink. And cut so it stands straight up. It's called punk, or something like that."

Elliott knew about punk, so he explained briefly while the others listened and said, "How odd" and "Really?" and when he had finished, Libby went on.

"And the other winner, the one who won second prize,

is a boy who goes to special education classes. You know, the classes for kids who have trouble learning."

"Hmmm!" they said and "Really, Libby?" She could guess the kinds of things they were wondering. Things such as what kind of a contest this had been and who had done the judging. The kinds of things Libby might have wondered herself if something hadn't happened that made questions of that sort seem unimportant.

"And *then,*" she interrupted their musing, making her tone of voice tell them that the most important part was about to come. "And then when we were all sitting there, in this little group, Ms. Ostrowski told Arnold Axminster that I was Graham McCall's granddaughter." She paused, searching their faces to see if they understood. If any of them even remotely understood the way she had felt.

They didn't. It was obvious that none of them did, not even Christopher. Taking a deep breath to relax the tension that was making her voice go high and quivery, she went on. "And Arnold Axminster said Graham McCall was a fine writer and that he was honored to meet his granddaughter."

"Were the other students all properly impressed?" Elliott asked, smiling innocently. Elliott could be very dense at times.

"Oh, Elliott," Libby said angrily. "Impressed! You can't impress people at Morrison Middle School with things like that. You impress people at Morrison Middle School by . . ." She stopped herself just in time. What she had been about to say would only have confused them even more, as well as giving away her secret and ruining her long-term plan. Instead she bit her tongue and then, after a moment, went on. "Well, anyway, then Mr. Axminster gave suggestions about how to prepare for a writing career. And one of his suggestions, the one he said was *the* most important, was that we should form a writers' workshop group that would meet regularly and criticize each other's work." Libby could hear her voice getting higher and shriller again. "And Ms. Ostrowski got all excited and said that we could use our Creative Choice time. You know, that's the hour on Wednesday afternoons when everyone goes to clubs or special lessons. She said that she'd see to it that the five of us could meet once a week and—" Her voice went higher still. "—And help each other with our writing."

They were beginning to understand now, at least a little. They were silent, their eyes full of concern. "But couldn't you tell Ms. Ostrowski that you'd rather not, if you feel so strongly about it?" Christopher asked finally. "I can certainly understand why you might not want to read your stories in public that way. But couldn't you say that you'd rather stay in your other club. Great Books, wasn't it?"

Libby shook her head. "No," she almost wailed. "I can't. Ms. Ostrowski had us vote, and all the others voted for it. I didn't think they would, but they did. Even Gary Greene. And Ms. Ostrowski promised Arnold Axminster. She promised him that she'd personally see to it that the five of us meet once a week for the rest of the school year."

Silence fell. Libby looked from face to face, trying to read their thoughts. Trying to guess if they were going to agree that it was impossible for her to continue to go to Morrison Middle School.

Christopher looked promising—worried and sympathetic. He was, she was pretty sure, on her side and since he

18

was her father, that certainly should count for a lot. But, on the other hand, Christopher was not at all good at making decisions. Sighing, Libby turned to the others.

Cordelia spoke first. "I, for one, am quite relieved," she said. "I really don't see what you're so concerned about. It's not as if you have to worry about not being up to the mark. I'm sure the whole group will be delighted with your stories. Delighted and astounded."

It was Libby who was astounded—that anyone, even Aunt Cordelia, could be so blind. Trying not to show her exasperation, Libby turned to Gillian. Surely her grandmother, who never agreed with Cordelia, would set Cordelia straight. "Gilly?" she prompted.

Gillian, who had curled herself up in her chair with her knees pulled up against her chest, in one of her typically ungrandmotherly poses, was grinning devilishly, showing her famous dimples. "You could write limericks about them. If they give you trouble, and it sounds to me as if you're afraid they might, you can give them back as good as you get. You write such clever limericks. Let's see. What does *pink* rhyme with? *Stink* comes to mind, but I'm sure you'll think of something more subtle. Yes, limericks. That's what I'd do if I were you."

Libby only shook her head, thinking that for once Gillian's advice was worse than Cordelia's. In desperation she turned to Elliott. He cleared his throat. "Well," he said briskly. "I must admit that I don't quite understand your anxiety about this writing group, but since you're obviously sincerely distressed, it seems to me that what we must do is to get you removed from the group. Perhaps your father could go to the school . . ." Elliott paused and looked at

Christopher, who was obviously not agreeing. "Or else I could go, and talk to this Ms. Ostrowski and—"

"No!" Libby said. "No! No! No! You don't understand. None of you understands anything." She was fighting back tears now, tears of anger and frustration. Pushing back her chair so violently that it nearly tipped over, she ran from the room.

3

Libby ran out of the dining room, leaving them all still sitting around the table. All of them just sitting there—so certain that there was some better way of solving the problem than the simple one of no more Morrison Middle School. Skidding to a stop in the center of the Great Hall—the enormous McCall House living room with its rough stone walls, soaring windows, and high vaulted ceiling—she found that she was panting, not from exhaustion but from anger. For a moment she considered running on—and on and on—doing what the family used to call her "exasperation run."

When she was younger, she had used running as a kind of safety valve. In those days, in fact even now in some circumstances, she had a quick temper, sudden and explosive, and when something she was working on just wouldn't turn out right—when an important experiment fizzled or a painting smeared, or when her legs and arms just wouldn't cooperate during ballet practice—she'd found she could race off her frustration and anger. And while Graham Mc-

Call's immense old house might not make much sense in many ways, it did make an excellent racetrack.

From the Great Hall she would burst out across the wide entry area and into the library. Gathering speed in the straightaway between the high bookshelves and the refectory table, she would career into Graham's study, a round room formed by the lowest floor of the tower. There, a quick spin around the huge old desk put her on the track to race down the window side of the library and out into the hall again.

The stairs came next, where a great deal of angry energy could be consumed by jumping up the wide, curving stairway two steps at a time. The poolroom and upstairs sitting room went by at full speed, but skillful cornering was needed to negotiate the long, narrow balconies that overhung the parlor.

Up on the third floor she would shoot down the narrow hall between small rooms that had once been servants' quarters but now held only Libby's private collections. The temporary ones (at the moment ancient Greece, the pioneers, and the British Empire) and the best and biggest and most permanent, her America in the 1930s collection.

The home stretch was a daring plunge down two flights of back stairs, to shoot out across the dining room and back to the starting point of the race. And it was a race, even though the only prize was an exhausted truce with herself, or with the cruel fate that sometimes seemed to spoil things just to make her angry.

Sometimes it was necessary to go over the course several times, and the family, sitting in the Great Hall or library, would look up each time she flashed by—curious but not particularly concerned. At least not since Mercedes consulted her psychiatrist and was told it was probably a healthy form of therapy, as long the runner was reasonably surefooted—which Libby certainly was. So they all went on calmly reading or talking, although now and then as she skidded around a corner or rocketed through a doorway, someone would call after her, "What went wrong this time, dear?" But she seldom stopped to answer, or at least not until she was forced to, paralyzed and calmed by exhaustion.

For a moment the urge was there, the old familiar need to do something headlong and full-tilt, but her feet refused to begin. Perhaps she was too old now. Or maybe it was because an "exasperation run" about the writers'-workshop catastrophe would be like admitting that it was no worse than those other unimportant little frustrations of her childhood. Instead she turned and with a slow, measured tread— a funeral procession or the march of the doomed to the gallows—went out into the hall and up the grand, curving stairway. On the landing, halfway up the stairs, she stopped long enough to tell her grandfather that she blamed him too.

Of course Graham McCall, who had been dead for over ten years, wasn't really there to be told in person. But his portrait hung above the landing, a life-size oil painting of the famous writer and world traveler, dramatically posed in khakis, jodhpurs, and pith helmet. When she was very young, Libby had held frequent conversations with Graham's portrait, long, involved discussions on every kind of subject. That was another habit she had more or less outgrown, except on rare occasions such as this, when she still had a few special comments to make to Graham McCall.

"It's all your fault, really," she told him. "At least it was to begin with. None of it would have happened if you'd just been something normal, like a farmer or a businessman."

But now, perhaps because of her own feelings of resentment, Graham's smile, which she had once thought kindly and understanding, seemed cold and mocking. Tossing her head, she glared at him angrily before she turned away and went on up the stairs, not even looking back, as she usually did, to watch the way the portrait's eyes seemed to follow as you climbed upward. At the top of the stairway she turned to the left, down the long hallway to her own room.

Libby's room, like everything that Graham McCall built during his years of fame and fortune, was extremely large. But unlike the rest of the house, where everything was just the way it had always been except for dust and wear and cat scratches, Libby's room was in a constant state of reorganization. Crossing the room, she wove a pathway between bookcases, tables, aquariums, terrariums, shelves, and easels, stopping only once to pick up Mercedes' letter— the most recent of the letters that arrived faithfully every week during Mercedes' absences and that, until recently, Libby had answered just as faithfully.

The letter began, *Hi there, my sweet sugar crumpet.* (Libby and Mercedes had made a private joke of thinking up ridiculous pet names to call each other.) *Why haven't I heard from you?*

"You haven't heard from me because it's your fault most of all," Libby said, giving the letter a punishing shake.

"I wouldn't even be going to Morrison if it weren't for you. That's why you haven't heard from me. Because if you hadn't come back here and told them that I needed to go out and learn about the real world and be 'socialized,' everything would be all right."

She shook the letter again, and her anger flared brighter, directed now most of all toward her mother, Mercedes O'Brien, who had gone away to live and work in New York City when Libby was three years old, returning only now and then—to criticize and interfere. Tossing the letter aside, she moved on to pick up a heavy jacket from the foot of her bed, shrug into it, and drop a small flashlight into its pocket. Then, prepared for the cool evening air and deepening dusk, she opened one of the French doors that led out onto the balcony.

Just beyond the balcony, growing up to tower even above the rooftops of the three-story McCall House, was the great oak, the ancient tree that had been there, already tall and stately, when Graham bought the land to build his castle. And where years ago, when Christopher was a little boy, there had been built a wonderful Treehouse. At this particular moment the Treehouse was Libby's destination—by a forbidden and dangerous route.

There was, of course, another way to arrive at the Treehouse, by a curving wrought-iron staircase that circled the oak tree's trunk. But the faster and more exciting pathway led up over the railing of Libby's balcony and then by a rather daring jump directly into a network of small branches. From there, if one was small and light and agile, one could climb carefully down to the fork that supported the first level of the Treehouse.

25

The Treehouse, Christopher's Treehouse, as the family still called it, was as large and strange (as overdone, as Gillian always said) as everything else that Graham built. The ornate iron staircase ended at a platform that surrounded the lower level, and from there the multilevel structure climbed up the forking limbs in a jigsaw puzzle of angles, ells, and projections, its exterior covered with a crazy quilt of rough-hewn shingles and decorated with oddly shaped panels and shutters.

Perhaps it was overdone and senseless, an enormous exaggeration of a treehouse, but it had been many strange and magical things to Libby: a bandit's hideout, a roc's nest, Tarzan's or sometimes Mowgli's jungle home, or even Baba Yaga's magical hut. Or just her private hideaway and refuge.

Today Libby made the climb down from the balcony quickly and carelessly. She was still breathing hard from anger and frustration as she pushed open the narrow door that led into the main room. Once inside, she shoved the door firmly shut behind her, leaned against it, and looked around. Here on the first level the interior walls were paneled and painted with scenes from myths and fairy tales; the paints faded, the figures dim and mysterious—even dimmer now in the evening light and faintly tinged with sunset purple. The few items of furniture in the room were mysterious, too, odd bits and pieces from Graham's travels, a bamboo bookcase, a chair made from a camel saddle, a jungle-drum table, and a small wooden settee, its seat piled with velvet pillows. The three stained-glass windows were oddly shaped —a circle, a triangle, and an octagon. In the far corner of the room a tiny twisted stairway led to the next floor, the bird room—a small, triangular-shaped area surrounded by all kinds of birdhouses and feeders. And above that on the third level was the circular lookout tower.

There was, there had always been, a feeling that went with stepping into the Treehouse and shutting the door behind her. A mysterious promise of good news—of magic to be revealed or wishes granted, or sometimes simply of peace restored.

Libby leaned against the door and waited—but now even the Treehouse failed her. Even here there was no escape from the memories of what had happened and, even more devastating, what would be happening soon. Collapsing among the pillows of the settee, she curled herself up into a tense knot of pain and rage. Her eyes tightly closed, she repeated accusing phrases over and over, holding on to her anger, knowing that when it went, it would be replaced by something worse.

Even when a plaintive yowling outside the door announced that Goliath had followed her to the Treehouse, as he often did, she refused to be interrupted or comforted by the big cat's warm and friendly presence. And when the fat old walking furball tried to climb up beside her onto the pillows, she pushed him away impatiently and went back to hoarding her fierce resentment. But in spite of all she could do, the armor of anger slowly oozed away—and, just as she had feared, the truth was there waiting.

The truth was—it wasn't really their fault. It wasn't their fault that they didn't understand. How could they, when she had been lying to them ever since her first day at Morrison Middle School.

After a while she sighed deeply, opened her tightly closed eyes, and sighed again. Then she slid down from the settee and, pushing aside the pillows, lifted the heavy seat to reveal a small metal file box. When the box was unlocked—by a key that hung around her neck on a chain—she took out a dark green spiral notebook.

She had many other journals. Some were the ordinary daily kind—reports on the progress of current projects, comments about books she was reading, and humorous accounts of the latest family battles, such as the endless one between Gillian and Cordelia, or Elliott's hopeless one with the cats—over whether furniture should be used as scratching posts. Some other notebooks were more or less special and private—such as the ones that held her short stories and novels. And one or two were top secret. It was only the top-secret ones that were kept in the old file box.

Leaning back against the settee, Libby pulled out her flashlight and, shining it on the green notebook—the one she had begun on the day she started school—she began to read, with her lower lip clenched between her teeth and her eyes squinted as if against a blow.

Elizabeth Portia McCall at Morrison Middle School
or
THE SOCIALIZATION OF LIBBY
First day:
Well, it's over. My first day "among my peers," as Mercedes would express it. My peers, it seems, are in seventh grade. At least, more or less. The counselor, Mr. Grayson, said that I was "academically prepared for eighth but that my age and size made seventh seem more appropriate." So it seems I'll be in eighth grade math and English classes, and seventh grade for everything else.

About size. I'm obviously not nearly large enough. It's partly my age, I guess, but actually I'm only about a year younger than the average seventh-grader, so part of it's just heredity. But for whatever reason, most of the boys are at least a foot taller than I am and the girls are closer to two. The girls are enormous. And nearly all of them have figures. I'm obviously too small and the wrong shape. I don't know why size should matter so much, though. Gillian says she has always liked being small.

I don't think I've made a great deal of progress on socialization yet. I tried to talk to a couple of people, but the con-

29

versation didn't progress very far. When I inquired about the subject matter that would be covered in the class, they either just laughed and walked away or said something like, "Are you for real?" And one boy said, "Hey, everybody. Look at this," and when everyone looked at me, he said, "I think you're lost, kid. The kindergarten is over on Eighth Street."

We didn't do much learning today. I guess that will occur later.

I'm going to like it, I suppose. At least, I told everybody here at home that I was. I'll just have to find some way to let my "peers" know that I'm more mature than I look. I'm going to have to work on that—showing them how mature I am.

Libby winced and quickly turned the page. The second page began:

I answered some questions in English today. Ms. Ostrowski, my English teacher—tall and willowy with beautiful cat eyes and a rather fiery temper—asked what a poet laureate was, and no one knew, even though the textbook tells all about it. So I explained about the laurel wreath and named a few of my favorite English laureates. And then I . . .

This time she flipped the page so hard it almost tore. Stupid! How could she have been so stupid. Why hadn't she been able to see right away what they were like? How much they hated anyone who knew more than they did, or was more talented, or who was different in any way. No wonder they'd started laughing and whistling every time she an-

swered a question. And calling her McBrain. No wonder
they started gathering around her between classes and asking her questions and then yelling and laughing when she
answered. And taking her books and putting them up out of
her reach on top of the lockers. If she'd only known enough
to keep her mouth shut—from the very beginning, instead
of waiting until it was too late.

With her hands still covering the notebook she rocked
back and forth, fighting down the angry waves. At herself
this time, for being so STUPID! Stupid to think that she
could impress people like that with how much she knew.
People who didn't know anything interesting or important,
and didn't want to. She shook her head hard. No, that
hadn't been it, at least not exactly. She hadn't just been
trying to impress them. What she had been trying to do was
simply to make them realize that she wasn't a dumb little
kid, even though she might look like one. What she'd been
trying to do, actually, was to make them like her.

Libby smiled. A bitter, ironical smile. Ironical because
all she had managed to do was to make them hate her. Not
that she cared anymore. She hated them, too. No, not hated
actually. Disdained was more like it. She disdained them for
being so stupid and boring and uninterested in anything
important, like the Great Depression, or the British in In-
dia, or poetry, or ballet, or anything—except each other.

After a few minutes she lifted her hands and looked at
what had turned up at random when she flipped the page.

OCTOBER 10,

Gary Greene imitated me again today during math class.
Actually he does imitations quite often. When the teacher is

31

late or if she has to leave the room, even very briefly, he always gets up and starts doing imitations. Usually he imitates Mr. Shoemaker, the principal, who walks in an odd way, with his toes turned outward. Or sometimes it's one of the teachers. But once he hugged some books up against his chest and scurried to his seat in a crouching position. Then he pulled up his feet and sat on them and held a book up on end and hid his face behind it. And everyone looked at me and laughed, and ever since then he holds his book up and hides behind it quite often, sometimes even when the teacher is in the room. No one will tell her what everyone's laughing about.

I know I sit on my feet sometimes, so I can see the blackboard over the heads of taller individuals. But I didn't realize I hid behind my book like that. And I DON'T walk that way!!

Gary Greene always shouts at me in the halls, too. Sometimes he bellows things like, 'Hey, McBrain. Want to do my homework for me? I'll make it worth your while.' Or, 'Here comes Little Frankenstein. All brain and no body.' Everybody laughs. By calling me Frankenstein he means, of course, that I'm a monster made of mixed-up parts, but that just shows how stupid he is. He obviously thinks Frankenstein was the name of the monster instead of the scientist who made him.

He's the monster. Gary Greene is a stupid monster!!!

"Monster," Libby whispered. "That's what I should have told Christopher when he asked about Gary Greene. I should have said, 'Gary Greene? Oh, he's just a stupid monster I happen to know.' "

She turned several more pages, skimming over the contents, and then on the fourth of November, there it was. The TRUTH. The real, true reason nobody, not Gillian, nor Elliott, nor even Christopher, was to blame for not understanding why she had to stop going to Morrison Middle School.

NOVEMBER 4,

Everybody was asking about school again at dinner tonight, and as usual I said everything was just fine. In fact I invented a new "best friend" to tell them about.

Sometimes I think that Christopher doesn't quite believe me. I'm not sure, because he probably wouldn't say so, even if he didn't. He's just that way. When I was little and I used to fib about things, I'd notice that he was just being especially quiet. And then I'd find out later that he'd known I was fibbing all along.

But the rest of them believe me, even Mercedes. Especially Mercedes. I guess she wants to believe that I'm doing just great at school because it was her idea in the first place. When she was here last month, she even gave me this little talk about how grateful I should be that she insisted on my starting public school, because I had made the transition so easily and well and if I'd waited another year or two, it would probably have been so much more difficult.

I really wanted to tell her the truth. I really wanted to tell her that I wasn't doing anything easily and well at Morrison Middle School and that all it was doing was making me miserable and that I wish she could be the one to be imitated and made fun of every day if she thinks that's what it takes to

33

be socialized. But I didn't, of course. All I did was agree with her and say how much fun I was having and how glad I was she'd talked them into sending me to school. It was really ironic.

I don't like lying to them, but I have to or my plan for the future will never work. My plan is to convince all of them— especially Mercedes—that one school year was enough to completely socialize me, so there won't be any reason for me to go back to Morrison next fall.

I know what would happen if I told them the truth. If I told them what it was really like, they'd be sure that Mercedes was right all along and that I'm hopelessly unsocialized. And that would mean they'd all be positive that I should stay in school forever. And it would be forever, because I know now that it's not going to get any better. At first I thought it might, but I know better now. They're never going to stop hating me.

Libby closed her eyes and shook her head. "Never," she whispered. It was some time later that she got up and pulled the camel-saddle chair up to the table.

It was almost completely dark by then, and it was necessary to hold the flashlight in her left hand as she opened the journal to the first blank page.

I guess there's no way out. I'll have to keep going to Morrison Middle School, and next Wednesday I'll have to go to the writing group. And I'll to have to read one of my stories to Gary Greene and those others.

Libby on Wednesday

She sat for a while staring blindly at the round spot
of wavering light before she sighed deeply and went on
writing.

*And then I'll come home and tell everybody how it wasn't
so bad after all, and how I really liked it. Otherwise they'll
make me go on being socialized forever.*

Recess had barely begun when Libby hurriedly opened the door to the reading lab. She had arrived early on purpose, reasoning that it would be worse to have to enter when the others were already there, just watching and waiting to stare and comment. The room was empty. She hadn't been aware of holding her breath, but as she stepped inside, her starving lungs rebelled with a hungry gasp.

The reading lab, a small classroom used for meetings and special lessons, smelled of books and chalk dust. There was a teacher's desk near the pale green blackboard, a scattering of student desk-chairs, and along one wall a number of large storage cabinets. Libby's only other visit to the reading lab had been on the day of the Literary Festival, when the winners of the writing contest had gathered there to meet with Arnold Axminster. Remembering that fateful meeting, Libby felt her teeth clench and her stomach tighten.

She had picked out a chair and was hurriedly moving it away from its closest neighbor, when a voice said, "Oh, it's just you." Libby gasped and whirled around in time to see a shaggy brown head emerging from one of the supply cupboards.

He came out of the cupboard in awkward angles, like an unfolding wooden puppet, and it wasn't until he finally untangled himself and turned to face her that she recognized him as the winner of the second prize. The one from the special education class. The tall, thin, jittery one with the nervous smile, which he was doing at the moment—a strange, twitchy grimace.

Sitting down in a clattering, loose-jointed collapse, in the seat closest to Libby's, he gestured by tilting his head back toward the cupboard. "That was just in case," he said. "In case of G.G." His voice had a jerky sound, too, almost —but not quite—a stutter.

Libby swallowed hard, and her own voice came out thin and wavering. "In case of what?"

"Who—not what. Our fellow prizewinner. Just in case G.G. turned up next, before there was anyone else here to witness the crime, if you know what I mean. You know who I'm talking about, don't you? G.G.! Gary the Ghoul. It's not common knowledge, but old Gary and I go way back. Way back to second grade. Real buddies we were then— briefly. Until he lost his temper over a missing Tootsie Roll he thought I'd eaten. Actually I hated the things, but he didn't believe me, so he pounded me into a pulp and threw me over the teeter-totter. And that was just the first time. The next time he really got rough. So you see why I wasn't about to risk being alone in a room when he . . ." He paused as the door slammed open and then went on in a whisper. "Speaking of you-know-who!"

It was Gary Greene. Two girls, the other two writers' festival winners, came in right behind him, but Libby barely noticed them. You didn't notice anyone else when Gary Greene walked into a room. He had a way of making sure of that. It wasn't because of his looks, that was certain. He was medium-sized, square and solid-looking, but not particularly tall, and his face was only normally homely for a person of his age and sex. And it wasn't just because he stomped and shouted a lot, either. Even when he walked softly and kept his mouth shut, the threat was there, in his dangerous smile and the way his eyes slid around—as if looking for prey.

"Hey! Hey!" he said loudly, grinning at Libby and the thin boy. "Look at this. We've got the wrong room. This must be the psycho ward." He turned to the two girls. "Look at this. What we got here is weirdo heaven."

Libby bent over her book bag, pretending she hadn't heard. But she had of course, and she also heard the laughter—a loud, squawking noise like a cackling hen. Glancing up through the curtain of her hair, she saw it was the big girl with the punk hairdo who had cackled. Someone else was laughing, too, but it wasn't the other girl. It was the thin boy himself.

"Ha, ha, ha," he screeched, "weirdo heaven." Then he jumped to his feet in an awkward explosion of motion, held his arms out dramatically, and began to sing in a high-pitched voice, "Heaven. Weirdo heaven. It's the place that only nerds and dorks can go. Aren't you sad that you can never know, what a—"

He stopped suddenly as Ms. Ostrowski burst into the room, apologizing in a loud, cheerful voice for being late.

Stumbling back into his seat, he opened a notebook and bent over it. For a moment the others—Gary Greene and the two girls—went on staring at him, and then, as Ms. Ostrowski chattered on, they turned slowly away. The thin boy's bent head turned toward Libby, and his mouth stretched into a brief, lopsided grin.

Libby's lips twitched in response before she quickly bent her head again over her notebook. As she stared blindly at the blank page, her mind raced. Where had the song come from? The tune sounded vaguely familiar, as if he'd just made up new words to a real song. Had he really made it up that quickly? How could he? And how *could* he jump up like that in front of the others and make a fool of himself?

As Ms. Ostrowski arranged six chairs in a circle, she kept up a steady stream of chatter, about Mr. Axminster and his wonderful suggestion to form a writers' workshop and about how much she was looking forward to being a part of it and on and on. While the teacher was talking, Libby watched the others—G.G. and the two girls—but mostly she watched the thin boy, who was perhaps crazy— or perhaps something harder to understand.

"So," Ms. Ostrowski said at last, when they were all seated, "Are introductions in order? I think most of you know that I'm Ms. Ostrowski, but since that's quite a mouthful, I'd like to suggest that you call me what some of my other classes do—and that is Ms. O. All right? And now about the rest of you. Do you all know each other?"

At first no one answered, but then the smaller girl, the one with sun-streaked hair and bluish eyelids, finally said, "I know Gary and Tierney, but I don't really know . . ."

She paused, and Ms. Ostrowski—or Ms. O—took over

again, telling everyone's name and grade and a little about the story each of them had written for the contest. The girl with the golden hair was Wendy Davis. Libby hadn't ever spoken to Wendy Davis, but she'd seen her many times before—on the stage with the student council and doing other student-leader things like introducing people at assemblies. She always looked—well, the way you were supposed to at Morrison Middle School, with the right kind of hair and clothes, not to mention size and shape.

Wendy, Ms. O said, had written a contemporary story about a group of teenagers and their interests and problems. When Ms. O said her name, Wendy looked around the group smiling and nodding at each person, even at Libby and the thin boy. Libby ducked her head and didn't smile back—not that she was afraid to. She just wasn't going to play that phony game. She had been at Morrison long enough to know that someone like Wendy Davis wouldn't smile at her and really mean it.

The other girl, the big one with the punk hairdo, was Tierney Laurent. As Ms. O announced that she wrote exciting detective stories, Tierney just scrunched down in her seat and looked the other way. She was dressed in what seemed to be several sloppy layers of expensive-looking clothing, and her legs were stretched way out in front of her. Her shoes were the black high tops a lot of people wore at Morrison. Except that the high lace-up shoes looked sharp in a stylishly ugly way on some people, and on the end of Tierney's large legs they looked like something a bag lady might wear. While Ms. O was talking about her story, Tierney kept her face turned away and her lips curled in a sarcastic sneer.

40

And then there was Gary Greene, who, according to Ms. O, had written a science fiction story. "Yeah," he said. "Like major action. Lots of blood and gore."

"Well," Ms. O said, "I think you're selling yourself short, Gary. There's a bit more to what you wrote than that, I think."

Then she turned to the thin boy. "And Alex," she said, smiling. "Alex Lockwood writes wonderful comedy. His entry in the Young Writers' Contest was a very funny parody."

"Parrotty?" Gary Greene said. "What's that, parrot language? Hey, Lockwood. You write in parrot language? Like, Polly want a cracker?"

Tierney snorted, but no one else laughed, and Ms. O was obviously angry, her green eyes flattened like an angry cat's. "That's not particularly funny, Gary," she said in a tight voice. "Nor very intelligent. Who does know what a parody is?"

Libby's mouth actually opened before she caught herself. "Yes?" Ms. O asked, but Libby only shook her head and went on shaking it as the teacher waited, smiling. "All right, then, I'll explain," she said at last. "For your information, Gary, a parody is a spoof, a lampoon. An exaggerated imitation of something. Usually something famous so that everyone recognizes what's being poked fun at. Alex wrote a very funny spoof of a popular horror story, Stephen King's *Cujo,* I believe."

For just a moment Libby was so caught up in Ms. O's explanation that she forgot to worry about what was coming next. So it was with a shock that she heard, "And our first-prize winner is Libby McCall, for a wonderful fantasy set in ancient Rome."

Libby kept her head down, and Ms. O quickly went on. "I think the first order of business today might be to think up a name for our group and then, perhaps, to set up our standard operating procedure. Does anyone have any good ideas about a name? Think about it for a minute or two, and then I'll ask for suggestions. Okay?"

Libby glanced around. Gary Greene was staring out the window and drumming his pencil loudly on the edge of his desk. Tierney was still slouched in her chair looking as if she were half asleep. But Wendy was bent over her desk chewing on the end of her pen and occasionally scribbling something in her notebook. As soon as Ms. O looked up, she raised her hand.

"How about the FFW?" she said.

"Standing for what?" Ms. O asked.

"Yeah, for what?" Tierney said. "The Funny Farm Writers?"

They all laughed, even Wendy. "No," she said. "What I was thinking of was the Future Famous Writers. You know, like, there's this Famous Writers Club, so we could be the Future Famous Writers."

Gary and Tierney both groaned but they didn't come up with any other suggestions, so Ms. O said that then it would be the FFW, at least for the present, so as to get on with the next order of business as quickly as possible—to set up an operating procedure.

In writers' workshops, Ms. O said, the participants sometimes read their material out loud to each other. But another way to go would be to make copies of each person's work for the other members to read ahead of time. Either way, the process would then be to take turns commenting on each story and offering constructive criticism.

"Constructive," she said, was the key word, and did they all know what "constructive" criticism was? They all said yes, but when she asked for examples, no one said anything—at least not at first.

But then Wendy Davis said it might be if you said something like, "I really think your characters are great, but it seems to me that you might need a little more work on plotting."

Ms. O liked that, but then she made the mistake of asking for an example of nonconstructive criticism.

Still slouched down in her chair, Tierney said, "How about, your characters are stupid and your plot stinks."

Gary laughed. "Yeah," he said. "Or your characters are putrid and your plot is double-dip barf."

After that Ms. O used up exactly five minutes threatening and scolding. Libby knew how long it took because she had been watching the clock closely, hoping desperately that the class would be over before it was her turn to read. Ms. O's lecture covered some generalizations about good citizenship and the sin of wasting the gift of a special talent, which was something—according to Ms. O—that all five of them certainly had. But then she went on to give some specific information about what might happen to anyone who behaved in a nonconstructive manner. Such as the fact that if people had to be thrown out of the workshop, they would spend their Creative Choice periods in detention. That part

43

of the threat didn't seem to impress anyone, but when she got around to saying that notes would also be sent to their parents, both Gary and Tierney seemed to take her lecture more seriously.

Watching Gary and Tierney sit up and stop grinning and sneering, at least for the moment, Libby found herself breathing more easily. If you had to be shut up in a room with those two, it seemed a little safer to have someone present whom they took seriously. Teachers, in Libby's experience, weren't always much protection, but in this situation it was a relief to see that Ms. O seemed to be in control.

There was a vote next, on whether to read out loud or make copies to pass around. While Ms. O was making some slips of paper for ballots, the thin boy leaned over and whispered to Libby.

"Let's vote to read out loud. Okay?"

"Why?" she whispered back. She had definitely been planning to vote for making copies. Having the others read her stories would be bad enough, but having to read out loud to them would be unbearable.

"Because—well, just because it would be more fun that way. Don't you think so? Besides, the other way you'd have to write your comments on their manuscripts, and I couldn't do that."

"Why not?" Libby said.

He grinned his twitchy, lopsided grin. "Because I can't write."

Libby was still staring at him in amazement when Ms. O handed around the slips of paper and the vote started. In spite of Alex's request, Libby voted the way she had intended to—to pass out copies—but it didn't make any difference. The majority was for reading out loud.

There was only about a half hour left in the period when Ms. O called on the first workshop member to read to the group. It was Gary Greene.

Libby walked home that day. It was only a few minutes by bus from downtown Morrison to the McCall House, and on foot it could take almost an hour, but she'd always preferred to walk. She liked strolling slowly down the long, shady streets and alleys lined with all kinds of houses, stopping now and then to look over fences, through hedges and into picture windows.

Looking into people's yards and houses was necessary, she had always felt, for a writer. A writer needed to learn how all sorts of people lived and the secrets they kept from the ordinary passerby. And yards, particularly backyards, often revealed that type of information. Libby knew of backyards in Morrison that absolutely swarmed with secrets. And so had her famous grandfather, Graham McCall. His books, particularly the ones set in Morrison, were full of fascinating backyard-type information.

So, walking through the streets of Morrison had always been important to Libby, even during the days of the Libby McCall Private Academy. But in the last few months it had become important in a different way. Sometimes, on her way home from Morrison Middle School, she simply needed some extra time to shake off the middle-school Libby McCall and get back to the person she used to be. To stop being the silent, angry McBrain—or Little Frankenstein—or whatever they'd thought of to call her on that particular day, and get back to being her old self.

The old Libby McCall. Sometimes it was hard to remember just who that had been. Thinking back, trying to imagine herself as she had been then, it sometimes seemed that she had never really thought about who she was, except in terms of what she was doing at the moment. Most often, of course, she had been Libby McCall, the writer. But then there had also been the actress, the dancer, the scientist, or the historian. Beyond that—beyond what she was writing or dancing or acting—she had just known, deep down, that she was simply Libby, and that had always seemed important and perfectly satisfactory. There had never been any reason to doubt it. Lately the changeover to that old Libby seemed to take longer and longer.

Today it seemed she would need that kind of between-worlds time more than ever. Making her way down Jefferson and Emerson and across Elm, she barely noticed the backyards, not even as she passed the Vincentis' house, where Mrs. Vincenti and her mother-in-law were, as usual, working in their vegetable garden and gossiping in loud voices about their neighbors.

Libby didn't even stop to listen. She had other things to think about. Walking slowly, her eyes straight ahead, her mind was busy with what had happened at the writers' workshop and with what she was going to tell them at home. What could she say that would not be too far from the truth and yet wouldn't make them even more sure that Elizabeth Portia McCall still needed years and years of socialization?

But instead of analyzing information and making logical plans, her mind kept jumping back and forth. Short bits and pieces of memories and emotions churned and tumbled, back and forth and over and over like clothing in a washing machine. At one point she remembered Gillian's suggestion that she write a limerick about the members of the group, and even though she knew they would never hear it, she began working on one in her head—a nasty, angry limerick, much worse than the ones she used to write about the family when she was upset with them.

She had almost finished the limerick by the time she pushed through the wrought-iron gate at the McCall House —and quickly forgot about it, as her mind went back to tumbling, without purpose or direction.

On the brick walk that curved to the front door through overgrown shrubs and tangled rosebushes, she walked more and more slowly. And at the foot of the broad, leaf-littered stone steps, she stopped altogether, as one useful idea emerged from the confusion. If Christopher were in the library, as he possibly would be at this time of day, he would be sure to ask questions like, "Well, how did it go?" or "How was the writers' workshop?" and that would be dangerous. She needed more time to plan, and besides, it would be better to tell them all at once.

Talking to her father alone would not be a good idea. With everybody present she could look mostly at Elliott, who always believed everything she told him, or at Gillian, who was always on her side whether she believed her or not. When you had to lie, it was better not to look directly at Christopher McCall while you were doing it—at least not if you happened to be his daughter, and very much like him in some important ways.

Back on the brick path she turned to her left and followed a trail that wound its way toward the east among the untrimmed and overgrown trees and bushes. After passing below the library windows and curving around the bulge of the tower, it skirted a huge Japanese quince and came to a stop at the foot of the Treehouse oak.

Writing would help. If she could have just a few more minutes by herself to write it all down. If she could put into words not only exactly what had happened but also just how she felt about it, perhaps it would all become clear in her mind. Writing had worked that way for her before. Writing a tantrum had taken the place of having one, and writing a confusion had sometimes cleared it up.

A few moments later, seated at the jungle-drum table under the pale timeworn eyes of the fantastical figures painted on the Treehouse's walls, she opened the green notebook and began.

FEBRUARY 25,

It was terrible! I hated it. I hated them all.

Slashing the *t*s and stabbing the *i*s so hard the paper tore, she sat back and stared at what she had written. It was working. She felt a little bit better already, and the limerick would help even more, if she could just remember how it

49

went. The first line had been about Tierney. Little by little it all came back.

THE FFW.

There's Tierney who's big, fat, and mean.
And Alex, the strangest I've seen.
And then there is Gary,
Who's cruel, dumb, and scary.
And Wendy who thinks she's a queen.

Reading it over, Libby found she was breathing hard. She read it again and then continued to bend over the table, her pencil poised, but nothing happened. It was several minutes before she began to write again—in short phrases—catching ideas that skittered through her mind—jotting down things almost before she had finished thinking them—tying them together with dashes.

GARY GREENE—*G.G.—Gary the Ghoul—Gory Gary—the reincarnation of someone horrible—like Hitler, maybe—or Genghis Khan—or an executioner during the French Revolution—he would have loved that—Gary Greene would have loved that old guillotine. His story was gruesome, too—all about a spaceman landing on a planet and killing all kinds of aliens in all kinds of gruesome ways—I don't see how he could have won even an honorable mention.*

She stopped again to think, her cheek resting on her fist, drumming the end of her pencil on the leather tabletop, letting her eyes roam around the dim figures in the wall murals: Robin Hood, Joan of Arc, Beauty and the Beast—

and Peter Pan, her favorite. Remembering how she used to talk to them when she was younger, how she told those palely brooding Treehouse companions all kinds of secrets, she picked up the notebook and read what she had written out loud. They seemed attentive, but when she had finished, they didn't, for some strange reason, offer any advice or criticism. Smiling—ironically—at her own childish behavior, she went back to drumming on the tabletop—and thinking.

Except—he does make his characters so you can see them—even if you don't like them—and you do know where they are and how they got there—I guess he does write better than a lot of the students at Morrison—which isn't saying much.

At the top of the next page she wrote:

TIERNEY LAURENT.

Taller than Ms. O—and a lot fatter—and almost as mean as Gary—acts angry all the time—sneers at everything —even at Gary Greene—after he read his story, she said it was boring—what she actually said was something like, "The first seven or eight massacres were just your average B-movie borrr-ring, but after that it was, I mean, what we're talking here is major ZZZs." But then she looked at Ms. O and said, "Oh, yeah. CONSTRUCTIVE! Something constructive about old G.G. That's a hard one. Oh, yeah. The icky green blood. I really flashed on that icky green blood. You got a really big imagination there, dude." Then she sneered again and said, "How's that for constructive?"

Ms. O asked Tierney to read her story next, but she didn't—said she'd forgotten to bring it—and Ms. O said okay but she better not forget next time, or else—and Tierney said, "Or else what?"—and Ms. O smiled and said, "Don't ask. You wouldn't want to know," and Tierney said, "Arrghh" and pretended to be terrified.

I don't think Tierney Laurent is dumb—definitely not dumb—just mean—and really angry about something.

And then there was Wendy Davis.

WENDY DAVIS.

She is a phony—always pretending—nicey-nice to every-body—when the teacher is around at least—that's probably how she got to be on the student council—by pretending she likes everyone—she didn't read today either because there wasn't time after Alex Lockwood.

ALEX LOCKWOOD.

The strangest person I've ever met—moves in a funny way—like a robot with mixed-up wiring—he's so afraid of Gary Greene he hides in the cupboard—and then he gets up in front of Greene and everybody and sings a crazy song—about dorks and weirdos—after Gary called him a weirdo—after he called Alex and me both weirdos.

Libby stopped writing then and began to drum again on the tabletop, beating out a definite rhythm this time, to a song that she halfway remembered.

That song—it was to real music—something I've heard before. And he must have just made up the words in a flash—with them all staring at him—I wish I could remember all of the words—I wish I knew how he did it.

He read his story, too, the parody of Cujo. *It was about a rabid chihuahua that had a bunch of people trapped in a car for years and years. The people in the car kept getting older and older—the little boy grew up and went through puberty, and the chihuahua was still drooling on the windshield and eating parts of the car, like the tires and the windshield wipers. Everybody laughed—even G.G. and Tierney.*

She thought for a while about Alex's story and how he had read it in a dramatic, quivering voice, like a parody of someone reading a horror story. And everyone HAD laughed. Everyone. Even Libby—at least a little. You couldn't help it.

What did he mean when he said he couldn't write?

On the next page she wrote:

I didn't have to read today—there wasn't time because Alex's story was so long—that was the best thing about it, in fact—but there were other good things about it—I mentioned some of them when Ms. O asked me to critique it—I said that I thought it was good how you got to know all the people who were shut in the car by the way they acted and the things they said, instead of just being told about them—and I thought he made the funny parts funnier because you halfway expected them after a while—like the way the dog kept eating another part of the car. Ms. O said she thought my critique was very good—and when I finished talking, someone said, "Yeah"—

like they were agreeing with me—I'm not sure who said it but it sounded like it might have been Tierney—and right after that the period was over.

Libby went back then and read over what she had written several times before she wrote in very large letters—

SO—

Then she drummed on the table and doodled stick figures up and down the margin of the page and checked out Peter Pan to see if he had anything to offer. At last she turned the pencil around and hurriedly wrote one last paragraph.

I'm sure it will be terrible—horrible—unbearable—next time when I'll have to read for sure, but this time—this time, it wasn't so bad after all.

And later, after the family had gotten through scolding her for coming home so late and worrying everybody, and then hugging and kissing her to make sure she knew they weren't really angry, they finally got around to asking her about the writers' workshop and how it had turned out. And that's just what she told them.

"It wasn't so bad after all," she said, and the funny thing was, it wasn't really a lie.

7

All through the following week, after that first meeting of the writers' workshop, Libby tried to prepare for the next Wednesday, when she would surely be the first one called on to read.

First and foremost she had, of course, practiced reading her story out loud. At various times during the week she read it with various amounts of dramatic expressiveness—sometimes to an empty room, at others to Goliath, who was always a quiet and attentive audience, and once even, in a humorous and ironical way, to her poor old fading Treehouse companion, Peter Pan.

She had also gone over in her mind the things Mercedes had told her about how actors prepared themselves for their entrances on opening night, in order to prevent attacks of stage fright—by eating candy or a spoonful of honey a few minutes before curtain time for a quick rush of energy and then by breathing steadily and very deeply just before going on stage.

So when the time came, and the day and hour finally

arrived, she felt that she was ready, or as ready as she was going to be. Arriving early again in the reading lab, she took her place in the farthest desk, took out her manuscript, opened it, and went on breathing deeply, while quickly munching a half-dozen jelly beans.

Ms. O arrived right after the bell rang. She smiled at Libby, said hello, and then sat down and began to go through some papers. Libby went on breathing deeply. Alex arrived a few minutes later, but the rest of them were very late that day, especially Tierney. Since Libby had begun the deep-breathing exercise as soon as recess started, she had been doing it for quite a long time by then, and it was just after G.G. arrived that she noticed that she was feeling strangely dizzy.

Something seemed to be spinning inside her head, and sections of Ms. O kept drifting back and forth as if she were on an out-of-focus TV screen—the wide cat-eyes drifting one way while the smiling mouth wavered off in another direction. It was an odd sensation, and Libby might have found it unnerving if she hadn't been a little too woozy to give it serious consideration.

But at last Tierney Laurent lunged through the door, slouched across the room, and collapsed into her seat, and Ms. O called the workshop to order. Sure enough, as soon as she had finished making a few pointed remarks about tardiness, she turned to look at Libby. Still feeling as if the top of her head wasn't quite connected to the rest of her, Libby tried to force her eyes to focus and her mouth to smile. But she must have looked as strange as she felt, because after a moment the teacher turned away—to Wendy Davis.

56

"Wendy," she said. "Are you ready to share your masterpiece with us today?"

Wendy's story, which was neatly bound and covered with a book jacket made of shiny pink cloth, was called "Robin in Pink." Libby probably would have groaned, silently of course, if she hadn't been feeling so light-headed. It sounded like the type of story that was all about teenage girls and their boyfriends and dates and parties, and what they wore to their dates and parties, and how they finally got the boy they wanted and the clothes they wanted and became the most popular girls in school. There were a lot of books like that in the school library, and Libby had tried a few of them—and found them boring. She felt her lips twitch. Borrrr-ing, she thought. I mean, we're talking major ZZZZs.

Wendy opened her neatly bound book, smiled at everybody, tossed back her pretty, sun-streaked hair, and bent over the first page. And as Libby prepared to listen, closing her own manuscript, tucking one foot up under her and leaning forward on her elbows, the dizziness gradually faded away.

In a clear, unhurried voice Wendy read:

" 'Robin in Pink,' by Wendy Davis.

"When the phone rang that Saturday morning, Robin Whitney just knew it was for her. Afterward she thought that it had probably been ESP, although her parents might have said it was only the law of averages. According to her parents, when the phone rang at the Whitneys' residence, it was for Robin nine times out of ten."

Wendy looked around at the group, her smile inviting them to be amused. No one seemed to be, but Libby found her lips returning the smile before she had time to decide not to. Wendy went on reading:

"But this time Robin sensed something was different. Somehow the moment the phone rang she knew something was wrong. Something important. And sure enough. The caller was her best friend, Heather, and the moment Robin said hello, Heather shouted into her ear, 'Have you heard about last night at the mall?'

" 'No,' Robin said. 'What about last night at the mall?'

" 'Jason was there with that new girl, Penny Johnson.' "

Libby tucked up the other foot and settled her chin on her fists. So far it was just about what she'd expected. The rest of the story was pretty predictable, too. Robin's boyfriend, Jason, was interested in another girl, and Robin would have to work out a way to get him back. Big surprise.

Wendy went on reading in her clear, steady student-leader voice about her heroine's tears and anger, and then, just as Libby had foreseen, about her PLAN to get her boyfriend away from the new girl. The PLAN centered around a big school dance. Robin was going to go to the dance wearing a sexy dress that would make her look so glamorous that Jason would forget all about the other girl. But then Robin's old grandmother made a dress for Robin to wear to the dance, a pink dress that Robin hated. Robin told her mother she wouldn't wear the dress, and they had a big fight.

The dialogue was good, particularly the fight between

Robin and her mother, and the characters seemed pretty real, but the ending was as predictable as the rest of it. The grandmother came down with a serious illness, and Robin decided she would wear the pink dress after all, for her grandmother's sake. And then, of course, the boyfriend loved the dress and the moment he saw Robin wearing it, he forgot all about the other girl.

"Well," Ms. O said, after Wendy said, "The End," and closed the pink book. "Who would like to comment first?"

Gary Greene made a gagging noise. Ms. O's eyes went fiery, and she was taking a deep breath, when he turned the noise into a cough. He went on coughing for several seconds and then held his throat and gasped. "Sorry. Bad cough, isn't it. You want me to comment first? Ooo-kay! Something constructive. Let's see."

Mugging a frantic expression with his lips pulled wide and his eyes rolling, he looked around the room as if he were asking for someone to come to the rescue.

"Constructive," he said. "Okay. Got it. The length. I liked the length of the story. For a story of that type it was just the right length. Not too long. That's all the comments I got. Okay?"

Tierney Laurent had raised her hand and was shaking it hard. When Ms. O finished staring at G.G. with threatening eyes, she looked at Tierney, hesitated, and then turned on to Alex Lockwood.

"Alex," she said. "Do you have any constructive suggestions for Wendy?"

Alex Lockwood squirmed, twitched his shoulders, shook his head, and then nodded it. He looked at Wendy and then at Ms. O and back again. "Well," he said finally.

"I think it wasn't confusing or anything. I mean, you knew what was going on all the time." He paused. "Of course, you pretty much also knew what was going to happen next. I guess that's what my suggestion would be. It was a well-written story, but maybe it could use some surprises. I mean maybe she could add something that would really surprise the reader." He stopped and thought a moment, and then his crazy grin jiggled across his face. "Like maybe Jason could like the dress so much that he falls in love with the grandmother—or something."

Wendy was looking down at her pink book, running one finger up and down the spine. Tierney Laurent had raised her hand again and was shaking it so hard that the spiky ends of her pink hair were quivering. "Mizzo," she kept saying. "Mizzo, call on me."

Ms. O looked at her doubtfully for a moment before she said, "Yes, Tierney?"

"I've got a lot of constructive comments," Tierney said. "Like G.G. said, the length was good. And I liked the pink cover a lot. And the way it had a title and characters and a beginning and an end. I particularly liked the way it had a beginning and end." She stopped and grinned. "It was just all the stuff in between that was dumb."

Peeking through her hair, Libby saw that Wendy's almost constant smile had disappeared. She looked hurt and surprised at the same time, like a slapped puppy or one of Gillian's cats that had just been stepped on.

Libby raised her hand. She didn't actually do it on purpose. It simply happened too quickly to think about, and when Ms. O nodded in her direction, she spoke quickly too.

"I think the story was very well written. Particularly

the dialogue. Like the fight Robin had with her mother. That was very real-sounding dialogue. It sounded like— like . . ." They were all looking at her and grinning. At least G.G. and Tierney were grinning. Libby's voice dwindled away to a whisper as she went on, "—like real people having a real fight."

"Yes," Ms. O said, "I quite agree. "I think that Wendy's story shows a great deal of writing talent. And while some of us might not be particularly interested in her subject matter, I think she handled the material very well." She glanced at the clock. "We're going to have to move right along if we're to finish hearing the other two stories. Libby, will you be next?"

Libby wasn't shaking as she opened her manuscript to the first page. Either she had simply gotten used to the idea or her anger about the comments on Wendy's work had burned away her fear. Her voice was only a little quavery as she began to read:

" 'Rainbow in the Dust,' by Libby McCall.

"The sun was low and the light was fading fast. Only a hazy glow slanted across the valley that stretched endlessly ahead of them. The people walked slowly, their heads bent low, their feet shuffling on the hard, dry earth. The only sound that rose above the dusty whisper of their feet was the occasional whimper of a child and now and then the hiss and thud of a centurion's whip."

She glanced up through her hair. They were listening. She took a deep breath and went on, her voice surer now.

"Too exhausted to fear even the cruel whip, Lucas trudged and stumbled forward, no longer aware of anything except that Pythia was still walking beside him, and that—"

Just at that moment the intercom squawked, and then Mr. Shoemaker's voice came on, announcing a change in the afternoon bus schedule. Someone, Libby wasn't sure who, made a groaning noise, and someone else, obviously G.G., muttered a four-letter word under his breath. And Tierney was sneering again.

Libby felt her face muscles contracting as if in anticipation of a blow. Although, on second thought, the groan and the sneer and even G.G.'s comment might just have been reactions to Mr. Shoemaker's interruption instead of comments on what she had read.

When the intercom clicked off, they all looked at Libby —and she went on reading. She read the part about the caravan spending the night among the ruins of the temple and how Pythia saw a vision of a beautiful winged horse. And even though Ms. O had said there would be a time limit of ten minutes, she went on reading until the caravan reached the slave market in Rome.

As soon as she stopped, G.G. started to say his favorite word. He got as far as "Shhh—" when Ms. O caught his eye. His voice trailed away, and then he grinned and started over. "Shhh-oot," he said. "You didn't write that yourself, did you, kid?" He looked at Tierney. "What do you want to bet that famous grandfather of hers wrote it for her?"

"Yeah," Tierney said. "Your grandfather write it for you?"

Libby felt a chill tighten her throat. It had happened

before, making her voice come out in a ridiculous squeak. Raising her head, she looked at Ms. O, asking for rescue. The teacher could tell them she'd written the story herself. Some of it had been written in the classroom for creative-writing assignments, and Ms. O had seen those parts in rough draft. But the teacher only smiled and nodded. "Yes?" she said, making the word a question, as if she, too, were wondering if Libby had had help.

Suddenly anger welled up, flooding her cheeks and melting the icy grip on her throat. There was no squeak in her voice when she said, "Well, if my grandfather wrote it, it must have been his ghost. He's been dead for ten years."

The screechy laugh was Alex Lockwood's. "A ghost-writer," he said. "Ghostwritten by Graham McCall. That's great. Why don't you send it to a publisher and tell them it was ghostwritten by Graham McCall? I'll bet they'd believe you. It's good enough."

"Yeah," Tierney said. "They sure would if they could see that spooky old house she lives in." She looked at Alex and then at G.G. as she went on. "You dudes seen that haunted house on Westwind that Graham McCall built? My folks are always taking tourist-type visitors out there to see it." Tierney pantomimed driving a car and gesturing grandly toward something beside the road. " 'There it is, folks, the famous McCall House, built by Morrison's most famous author.' And then everybody always says how it looks deserted. But it's not. You live there, don't you, shrimp?"

Ms. O had been saying Tierney's name over and over again in a stern tone of voice, and at last Tierney stopped talking. Everyone was staring at Libby.

"Do you?" Wendy was looking very excited. "I love that house. Do you really live there?"

Libby nodded. "It doesn't look deserted on the inside," she said. "Or in the backyard. It's just that it's so big and old and no one has the time—"

"Oh, you're so lucky. I think that would be a wonderful place to live," Wendy said. "Do you—do you suppose I could see the inside of it someday? I've been imagining it forever."

"Yeah," Tierney said. "Me too. I'd like to see it, too."

They were all agreeing, asking if they could see the house, and Ms. O was saying "People! PEOPLE! Let's get back to work," when the bell rang for the end of the period.

"So, we'll start our next session by finishing the critique of Libby's story and then we'll go on to Tierney's," she said. "That will be the last of the stories that were entered in the writing contest, so I hope you're all working on something new to share with us."

They all said they were. Alex said he had "tons of stuff —boxes—barrels—libraries full," and when Libby said, "So do I," he grinned at her and said, "I'll bet you do."

As soon as Ms. O left the room, Libby hurried out, too, not wanting to be left alone in the reading lab with the others. But out in the hall Wendy ran after her. She caught up just as Libby got to her locker.

"Libby," she said. "I didn't get a chance to tell you. I think your story was just—just outrageously awesome."

"Outrageously awesome?" Libby asked.

"Yes," Wendy said. "Great! Wonderful! Tremendous! Outrageously awesome." She was doing her bright and shiny student-leader smile right at Libby. At least it was right at Libby for a second, until it shifted to some people who were coming down the hall. Then she yelled, "Hey! Wait for me," and ran off after her friends without even saying good-bye.

As Libby opened the locker and put away her manuscript, she was thinking—outrageously awesome. "Outrageously awesome," she whispered to herself—and then, "or else—she just wants to see the inside of my haunted house."

8

That afternoon Libby took the bus home, although the weather was perfect, with a cool spring sun sparkling on a sleek, rainwashed world. There was even a special reason for walking on that particular day—in order to check out the Vincentis' backyard, where the two Vincenti ladies had been planting tomatoes recently and having interesting conversations about the divorce that was happening next door. But for some reason Libby had simply hurried to the bus stop without stopping to ask herself why and arrived at the McCall House much earlier than usual.

It wasn't until she was prowling around the house looking for someone to talk to that she made the connection. For once she had something really good—and really true—to tell them about.

No one was in the library or Great Hall, but there were two letters addressed to Libby on the enormous redwood burl coffee table in front of the fireplace. The first one, from Mercedes, Libby jammed into her jacket pocket, knowing pretty much what it would say without reading it—that in a light, kidding way it would ask her why she wasn't writing. And then at the end, after a few paragraphs about how the play was going and the funny things that had happened backstage, it would wind up with another little hint that Libby hadn't written for a long time.

The other letter was from Felicia, whose mother worked for Elliott in the bookstore. Felicia had been Libby's special friend for several years, coming over often to help work on the collections, to play chess, or just to talk about books and writers. But last fall Felicia went away to college. Libby quickly opened the letter and skimmed it—mostly about classes and professors, and then stuffed it, too, in her pocket —and went on looking for someone to talk to.

The first person she found was Elliott in the kitchen. Surrounded by a ring of attentive cats, he was bending over the huge old Wolff range, stirring something that smelled delicious.

"Hi, Elliott. Aren't you home early?" she said, as she maneuvered between cats on her way to the refrigerator, stopping long enough to pat heads or scratch ears. "Hi, Ariel. Salome. Isadora. Greetings, Goliath, you fat old thing."

"Ahh, Libby," Elliott said. "You're just in time. Come taste this for me and tell me what you think. Perhaps a bit more curry?"

While Libby tasted, and then tasted two or three more times, because Elliott's curried chicken was delicious and she was starving, he explained that Janice had taken over for the afternoon so that he could come home and cook. Janice was one of Elliott's employees, the one who was Felicia's mother. She had been a good friend of the McCalls for years and years, and taking over so that Elliott could come home and cook was one of the nice things that she often did.

"Business was slow today," he said, "and I had a sudden culinary attack."

Libby grinned around a mouthful of hot curried chicken. Calling Elliott's frequent urges to cook something special a "culinary attack" was part of a family joke. The rest of the joke concerned how completely uncontagious his "attacks" had always been. Even though Elliott had lived with the McCalls for almost six years now, no one else in the family had shown any signs of catching the disease. They had, in fact, gone right on being as hopeless in the kitchen as ever. And, although she had been quite young in those pre-Elliott days, Libby could remember just how hopeless that had been.

After Mercedes had given up on being a Californian and moved back to New York, the rest of the family had decided to take weekly turns shopping and cooking—with disastrous results—one week as disastrous as the next. When it was Gillian's turn, it was feast or famine—lobster and caviar until the money ran out. When Cordelia shopped, she bought only things that everyone hated—on the grounds that such foods were probably better for you and would certainly last longer. And Christopher tended to buy mysteriously inedible things with poetic names, like plantain and aubergine. But then Christopher was invited to the poetry reading at Elliott's store, and soon afterward Elliott moved in—and wonderful things like chicken curry began to happen in the McCall kitchen.

"Umm," Libby said, taking another taste. "Outrageously awesome. Which reminds me. Today was the writers' workshop."

"Yes, I know," Elliott said. He wiped his hands on the front of his apron, a long canvas affair with a coat of arms with crossed shish kebabs on the stomach, poured himself a cup of coffee, and eased his long, lanky body down into a kitchen chair. "I've not forgotten. How did it go this time?"

Libby poured a glass of milk and joined him at the table. "I read my story," she said, and paused for effect. "AND THEY LOVED IT." A slight exaggeration perhaps —but the rest of it wasn't. "Wendy said it was outrageously awesome," which was the absolute truth and Wendy's exact words. Why she said them was another matter, and one that didn't need discussing at the moment.

There was no need, for instance, to mention that the workshop members wanted to visit the house, because they weren't going to get to. Not that Libby wouldn't be permitted to invite them. Without even asking, she pretty much knew what the family would say.

Gillian would think it was a wonderfully exciting idea. Cordelia would certainly approve if it could be done properly with formal invitations and suitable refreshments. Elliott would say it wasn't up to him to decide, since he was only an unofficial McCall House resident. Only Christopher might be more or less against it, simply because he was such a private person. But, on the other hand, Christopher almost never insisted on having things the way he wanted them. So the vote would be two yeses, one "I suppose so if it's really important to you," and one abstention.

However, there wasn't going to be a family election because the most important vote—Libby's own—was NO. A loud and definite NO. And even though Libby hated to admit it, even to herself, Elliott was one of the main reasons for that NO.

It wasn't that Elliott wasn't a great person and a terribly important member of the family, because he was. But it was just that he was one more thing that didn't fit in to the usual pattern. How many people had an extra adult male family member who was not at all related to anybody? And anything at all unusual was just one more thing for people like G.G. and Tierney to make fun of.

Elliott was delighted with Libby's account of the workshop meeting, and Christopher was, too, when he came in from the garden a few minutes later. And at dinner that night, while everyone had an outrageously delicious meal of chicken curry with mango chutney and condiments, there was quite a bit of discussion about how glad everyone was that Libby's reading of her story had turned out to be such a success. Libby was feeling pretty good herself, although in the back of her mind there was still a little prickling reminder that the jury was still out on just how successful she had been. There was something else that kept prickling there, too, and after dinner some of it came out in a very roundabout way. She was talking to Gillian at the time.

It was dark by then and raining again, hard and steadily. The wind roamed up and down the long, cavernous verandas of the McCall House, pounced around corners, and drove sheets of water against the tall windows of the Great Hall. It was the kind of night that suited Graham McCall's castle, the dim shadows hiding its shabbiness and the noisy threat of the wind and rain making it seem a safe, strong fortress against the storm.

Libby on Wednesday

Christopher had built a fire in the Great Hall's huge stone fireplace, and Libby and Gillian were reading in front of it, curled up together in one chair. One chair was all that was necessary, since Graham's custom-built leather furniture was so huge and Gillian and Libby were both so small and loose-jointed. It was quite possible, in fact, for one chair to hold all four cats as well, although tonight there was only Salome, curled up in Gillian's lap, and Ariel, draped over Libby's armrest.

Gillian, who was wearing her favorite black sateen harem pants and a madras cloth tunic, was reading a book by Muriel Spark. And Libby, in her usual jeans and T-shirt, was reading a beautiful new book on Greek mythology that Elliott had just brought home from the store.

"Gillian," Libby asked suddenly. "Do you suppose we could afford to have something done about the front of the house?"

"The front of the house?" Gillian marked her place in the book with one finger. "What's wrong with the front of the house?"

The same question had occurred to Libby, but having made a special inspection just before dinner, she now thought she knew. In fact it seemed strange that she hadn't noticed it before.

"Well, it's looking awfully run-down, don't you think? The yard's so overgrown and the balconies need painting. And some of the shutters are crooked. It almost looks deserted, like a haunted house, or something."

"Oh, that," Gillian said. "I suppose you're right. I hadn't thought much about it."

"Well," Libby said. "This friend of mine at school said

something about it." Referring to Tierney as a friend wasn't easy, but she managed to get it out. "What she said was that her parents are always bringing people here to see it and they always say it looks like a haunted house."

Squeezing her way past Ariel, she got to her feet and began to act it out the way Tierney had done—being one of Tierney's parents pompously pointing out the home of the famous writer. Then she added her own original touch by moving backward to indicate a backseat passenger, peering out big-eyed and saying in an excited voice, "Oh, my, is it really? Oh, I'm so excited! Is that really where Graham McCall lived? But why does it look so deserted? Do you suppose it's haunted?"

Gillian applauded, waking Salome, who mewed accusingly before she rearranged herself and went back to sleep. As Libby climbed back into her corner of the chair, Gillian regarded her thoughtfully for a moment before she said, "We might discuss it with Christopher. It seems that he might do something about the yard at least, since he enjoys gardening so much."

"I know," Libby said. "He loves to garden—in the backyard."

Ever since Libby could remember, Christopher had spent a great deal of time out-of-doors, mowing and pruning and planting the three large terraces that stretched from the back of the house clear down to the river's edge. And when he was finished, he often sat on the highest terrace in the garden gazebo—a Graham-built gazebo, large and ornate with a peaked and pinnacled roof and glassed-in walls— where Christopher wrote poetry or simply enjoyed the results of his hard work in the garden.

And the results were beautiful. The backyard of the Mc-
Call House was every bit as grand now as it had been in the
days when Graham McCall was alive. It was only in front
that . . .

"I wonder why Christopher never . . ." Libby began
and found that Gillian was saying exactly the same words.
They both laughed, and after they'd thought for a moment,
they laughed again and nodded, because of course they really knew the answer. The backyard of the McCall House,
sheltered as it was by high fences and hedges, was a se-
cluded and private place. To work in the front yard, on the
other hand, would invite the stares not only of chance pas-
sersby but also of the dozens of people who made special
trips to stare over the fence at the famous McCall House,
the enormous old stone mansion built by Morrison's much-
beloved or (depending on your point of view) despised
author.

"Christopher couldn't stand that," Gillian said, as if she
had been reading Libby's mind.

Libby nodded. "Why?" she said after a while.

Gillian ran her hand through her pixie-cut gray hair.
"Why, indeed," she said. "He certainly didn't get his retir-
ing nature from his father—or from me. But he's always
been that way, quiet and shy except around people he
knows well. But sometimes I think it was our fault,
Graham's and mine. When Christopher started to go to
school, Graham's books set in Morrison had just come out
and, as you know, not everyone was pleased. Some of the
local residents accused him of spreading slander and gossip,
and for a while there was even talk of lawsuits. Nothing

came of the suits, and of course nowadays no one cares about such things anymore."

Gillian smiled an ironic one-dimple smile and then went on. "I gather that some of the people who complained then that Graham had ruined their reputations are rather proud of it nowadays—now that ruined reputations are so much more popular."

But after a moment even the ironic smile faded, and Gillian sighed. "However—Christopher did have a hard time for a while, and sometimes I think that to send a small, sensitive boy to school in a town that has a grudge against his family is a rather foolish thing to do. Christopher didn't complain very much, but I know that he wasn't happy for a long time."

"Umm," Libby nodded. She'd heard about it before, how much Christopher had hated going to public school, which was probably one of the reasons he'd agreed to having her taught at home for so long. Not that he'd expected her to have the same kinds of problems. "I was always such a shy, tentative child—not at all like you," he'd told her before she started school. "I'm sure you'll have no problems at all." And Libby had pretty much agreed with him—until her first day at Morrison Middle School.

They went back to their books then and read quietly for several minutes before Gillian asked, "What made you think about it, the front yard, I mean? Was it just what someone said about bringing visitors by to look at the house, or had you been worrying about it before?"

"No. Not before. It was just what Tierney, this friend of mine, said, I guess, that made me think of it. I don't think I thought much about it before that."

74

Gillian nodded and opened her book. But before she'd had time to get really into the story, Libby interrupted again.

"What do you think people say about Mercedes? I mean, don't you think people say it was wrong of her to go back to New York and leave Christopher and me here?"

"Oh, I don't know," Gillian said. "What do your friends say about it? About having a mother who lives someplace else most of the time?"

"Nothing," Libby said. "That is, most of them don't know. I don't talk about it much. But if some of them came here, they'd probably ask where my mother was, don't you think? And why she went off and left me?"

Gillian nodded thoughtfully. "Well, I imagine they're quite accustomed to the idea of parents who live apart, in the case of divorce."

"I know. But this is different, isn't it? Christopher says he and Mercedes never considered divorce. He says they've always been very good friends."

"That's quite true," Gillian said. "And it's also true that they've been even better friends since Mercedes has been spending most of her time on the East Coast. But I understand what you're saying. It is more unusual for a mother to leave her family in order to carry out her chosen career. But I think you know how I feel about it. Acting is a 'calling,' just as writing or dancing is a 'calling,' and I don't think anyone can be blamed for following a 'call.' "

Libby hung her head, studying her fingernails. She knew that was what Gillian would say—that she wouldn't blame Mercedes. She herself had never blamed her, until recently. When she was younger, she had always felt it was a decided advantage to have a mother who lived in an exotic place like New York City and acted on the stage, and came home suddenly at unexpected times bringing gifts and all kinds of exciting stories, and making up for being gone so long by being particularly full of good ideas about exciting things to do. But she blamed her now—for Morrison Middle School —but that, of course, was not something she could say to Gillian.

Libby sighed. "Well at least she didn't leave until I was civilized enough so I wouldn't be too much trouble for the rest of you to take care of."

Gillian laughed and hugged Libby's shoulders. "My dear child. You were never any trouble. And as for being civilized—at the age of three and a half you were in many ways the most adult member of the family—until we got Elliott, anyway. And besides, no one could say that Mercedes deserted us. Not when she always comes back between jobs."

"I know," Libby said. "I was just thinking about what some people might say."

Gillian put down her book and took Libby by both shoulders and gave her a little shake. "What people might say?" she said. "Will you listen to yourself, child. You sound just like Cordelia."

Libby smiled. It was true, in a way. True at least that Cordelia was always worrying about "what people might say." But this was—different. "This is different," Libby told Gillian.

"Different?" Gillian asked with her one-dimple smile. "In what way?"

"Well, it just is. It's different because I'm not *worry-*

ing about it the way Cordelia does. I'm just—thinking about it."

And that night in bed she thought about it some more as the storm, still raging outside her windows, sent anxious shadows scurrying around the room and then into her dreams.

During the next week Libby had something new to worry about—the fact that the discussion of her story would be the first thing on the agenda at the writers' workshop's next meeting.

Sometimes she felt confident. After all, Wendy had liked it, and Alex had more or less said that it was good enough to make a publisher believe that it was written by Graham McCall. That only left Tierney and G.G. ONLY? That was really ironic. That was, without a doubt, the largest only in the whole world.

At other times she felt—or tried to convince herself that she felt—unconcerned. After all, what if Tierney and G.G. were horrible? It would only be what one had to expect, considering the source. "Considering the source" was a favorite phrase of Cordelia's. The sources that Cordelia usually had to consider were stupid clerks or rude taxi drivers, and what Cordelia obviously meant was that you simply couldn't expect anything better from "such people." And, Libby told herself, you certainly couldn't expect anything better from such people as Gary Greene and Tierney Laurent.

But in between the short spells of feeling almost confident or almost unconcerned, there were the other, longer times when small dark moments of dread whispered through her mind.

The week seemed much longer than normal, but Wednesday arrived at last, and Ms. O called the third meeting of the Future Famous Writers to order by announcing that the first event of the day would be Tierney's reading of her prizewinning story. Apparently everyone, including the teacher, had entirely forgotten that there hadn't been time to finish the discussion of *Rainbow in the Dust*.

To her amazement Libby found that she was as disappointed as she was relieved. Not to mention a little bit angry. By the time she'd gotten control of the confused tangle of dread, relief, disappointment, and anger, Tierney was well into her story. Frowning fiercely as always, she was crouched over her manuscript and reading fast, in a loud, threatening voice.

"The next morning I got to the office late, but not late enough. My head still felt like a bass drum in a Fourth of July parade. My footsteps thundered, the door hinges shrieked, and even the sunlight was too noisy. I eased into the room and pulled down the blinds. I was quietly lowering myself onto my swivel chair when the door opened fast and hard. The sound throbbed like a tin drum in an echo chamber. Holding my head with both hands, I opened one eye.

"She was tall, with a face that belonged on a magazine

79

cover and a body that rated a centerfold. Her smile was an invitation.

"I opened the other eye. 'Hatchet,' I said. 'Rafe Hatchet. Private Eye.' "

At first Libby thought she had read it before. All those famous detective stories were in Graham's library, books written in the thirties by people like Dashiell Hammett or Raymond Chandler. Libby had read nearly all of them and had taken some of the most famous upstairs to be a part of her thirties collection. But as Tierney went on reading, she wasn't so sure. It wasn't so much exactly like a particular story as quite a bit like a lot of them.

As the story went on, it turned out, of course, that the beautiful girl needed a detective. Her brother had mysteriously disappeared, or that's what she said, at least. So Rafe Hatchet took the case and, right away, people started being killed. A policeman was shot, a mysterious man burst into Rafe's office with a knife in his back, and finally an old friend of Rafe's was strangled.

For a while Libby was busy asking herself which incident came from which book. Most of them sounded vaguely familiar but she couldn't quite place them, since some of the original stories had blurred together in her mind. But when it came to the ending, there was one thing she was certain about. That was when it turned out that the beautiful girl herself was the murderer. That one was right out of *The Maltese Falcon.*

It wasn't until the story ended that Libby suddenly realized that she'd been so busy listening and trying to remember where she'd read each part before that she'd forgotten to think about some other important considerations. Considerations such as what constructive remarks could be made about Tierney's story. And how in the world Tierney Laurent happened to have written a detective story that sounded as if came right out of the thirties.

She had just begun to deal with the question of what her comment would be when she noticed that Alex was shaking his hand in the air and grinning all over his face. "Mizzo," he kept saying. (Everyone was calling her Mizzo now.) "Mizzo. Call on me."

Ms. O laughed. "Well, Alex. Since you seem to have something urgent to say, I guess—"

But before she could finish, there was an interruption—a loud one.

"Hey, Laurent," Gary Greene said. "Where do you get off talking about my stuff having too many killings? You got as many as I do."

Tierney's eyes narrowed, and her spiky hair quivered. "I do not!" she yelled. "You had a lot more. I counted. You had at least twice as many."

"Yeah! Well, so what. Yours are at least twice as boring."

Tierney's jaw jutted and her eyes were down to slits, and for once she was sitting up straight. Unwound from her usual slouch, she looked amazingly tall, and angry and dangerous. "Oh, yeah! Well, let me tell you something. This—" She slammed her manuscript down on her desk. "—This happens to be a classical detective story, and in detective stories you have to have murders. And unlike the senseless gore in some people's junk, my murders have something to do with the plot of the story. And besides that . . ."

G.G. was talking at the same time, yelling something about laser guns and disintegrators being a lot more exciting than out-of-date stuff like knives and guns, and Mizzo was shouting "Tierney! Gary! That's enough."

When they finally stopped yelling and were just sitting there glaring at each other, Mizzo shook her head and sighed gloomily. "I'm certainly glad that Mr. Axminster isn't here to see what's happening to this group that he had such high hopes for," she said. And then she went off into another lecture about how sad it was to see five such *incredibly* talented and intelligent young people who had so much to offer and yet had so much difficulty relating to each other and each other's work—and so on and so forth. It wasn't until she'd covered the subject very thoroughly that she turned back to Alex.

"What was it you wanted to say, Alex? Or have we made you wait so long that you've forgotten?"

He hadn't forgotten and he was still squirming with excitement. "Yes," he said. "I mean no. I mean, what I wanted to say was that I thought it was great. And I thought I was the only one who wrote parodies. How come you didn't say you did too?"

Tierney's scowl, which until that moment was still focused on G.G., turned toward Alex. "What do you mean, parodies? I don't write parodies."

Alex looked startled, and unbelieving. "You mean, that wasn't a parody? I thought—well, it seemed to me like a great parody of—"

"Well, it wasn't!" Tierney sizzled between clenched teeth. "It's a detective story. My detective story. It's not making fun of anything. It's an original detective story."

"Oh, well, okay," Alex said, looking embarrassed. But then his jiggly smile seeped out through the embarrassment. "You mean all that great stuff like his name—you know, Hatchet—as in Spade, Hammer, and Cannon and like that. You mean that isn't . . ." His jittering eyes paused for an instance on Tierney's white-hot scowl, and his voice trailed away. "Okay. Okay," he finished. "My mistake."

It occurred to Libby that she could see what Alex meant. It could very well have been a parody, and a pretty good one too. But whether it was or not, there was something else about it that she found fascinating. A lot of things actually. People and places and events that Tierney had mentioned in her story. Her hand shot up, and almost before Mizzo nodded, she started asking Tierney how she knew about some of the things in the story, things like Laurel and Hardy, and Packard cars, and the World's Fair in San Francisco. Tierney stopped frowning at Alex and looked at Libby suspiciously for several seconds before she shrugged and said, "I like all that old stuff—you know, like before the Second World War. I read about it a lot and I collect stuff too. It's kind of a hobby."

"Mine too!" In her amazement, Libby forgot to work on keeping the squeak out of her voice, or even to notice if it was there. "Mine too. I have a whole collection of things from the thirties at home. Books and pictures and phonograph records and a lot of other things."

"Yeah?" Tierney suddenly looked different, almost like someone else. It took Libby a moment to realize that the difference was that, for once, she wasn't frowning. "So do I. And films too. I got lots of old movies on video. Black-and-white. I've got a lot of Marx Brothers, and Laurel and Hardy, and a real early Shirley Temple."

"And Big Little Books," Libby said. "You know, those fat little books with lots of pictures like they used to have in the thirties. I have a lot of Dick Tracy and Tarzan, and some—"

"Yeah? Really? Big Little Books? Great! I've been looking for those in old bookstores for a long time, but they're real scarce. Maybe we could trade. I'd trade you a movie for some Big Little Books if they're real good ones."

"Girls," Mizzo said. "Girls!" She sounded stern, but she was smiling. "If you could postpone this transaction until after class, perhaps we could get back to the business at hand. Wendy. What do you have to say about Tierney's story?"

Wendy turned her face slowly toward the teacher and smiled her confident, shiny smile. "Yes," she said, and then she shook back her wavy hair and rolled her eyes thoughtfully. Libby watched her with interest, wondering about the way she took her time, even though everyone was looking at her and waiting. At last she smiled again and said, "Well, I think Tierney's story is, like, a good example of a certain kind of detective story." She turned and smiled at Alex. "You know, just like Alex said. It was just such a good copy of that kind of thing. I don't read much of that kind of book but I've seen the movies on TV, and the people talk just that way—you know, tough-guy-sounding and very short sentences." She paused and smiled again at Mizzo. "I think Tierney did a really good job of copying those old-fashioned detective stories."

Tierney was scowling again like crazy. G.G. was grinning, and Alex's eyes were darting from Wendy to Tierney and back again. Alex's mouth wasn't laughing, but something else in his face was. He turned his face toward Libby and twitched the corners of his mouth before he whispered so softly that she almost had to lip-read. "Revenge. Sweet revenge. Sugarcoated, in fact."

When Wendy finished, Mizzo looked at her sternly for a moment as if she were trying to decide whether to bawl her out for being unconstructive, but Wendy just went on smiling her doll-faced smile and Mizzo finally stopped scowling. Libby didn't blame Mizzo for letting herself be fooled. It was hard to believe there was anything nasty behind a smile like Wendy's.

After that Mizzo did her own critique on Tierney's story by saying that it was a very professional job in many respects, with a well-planned plot and lots of action. But then she went on to say that she would have to agree that it did seem to be a little bit derivative.

Mizzo went on, then, all about how good all the stories had been, and while she was talking, Wendy poked Libby and whispered, "Derivative?" Libby whispered back, "Well, 'copied,' but more polite," and Wendy smiled not quite as sweetly as usual and said, "I thought so."

No one else had time to read that day. Mizzo went on for quite a while about how good all the prizewinning stories had been and how much she loved working with such a talented bunch. "Incredibly talented bunch," she said actually. Mizzo tended to use the word *incredible* a lot, particularly when she was talking about the Future Famous Writers. Then she said she was going to tell them a secret.

The secret was that Mizzo herself was a writer. A closet

writer, she called herself, and she had been working on a novel for more than two years. It was a secret, Mizzo said, because she didn't want the rest of the school—the other faculty and Mr. Shoemaker particularly—to know until she was published, if that ever happened. She was hoping to finish the rough draft by the end of the school year and she already had an agent who thought he could sell the book as soon as it was finished. Libby wasn't surprised. There was something about Mizzo's intelligent cat eyes and the expression in them when she talked about writing that pretty much gave it away.

After that Mizzo talked about some of the techniques she used for her own writing, and one of them was what she called her character chart. She had made up the chart for her own use, to remind herself to think of all the things she needed to know about the people in her stories. But now she had decided it might be a useful device for the members of the FFW, so she passed out several copies to each of them.

The chart listed all kinds of physical characteristics, such as eye and hair color, height and build, as well as dozens of mental and emotional traits, such as *intelligent, treacherous, practical, kindhearted, aggressive,* and *bad-tempered.* There were boxes to check the ones that applied to each character and a place to write a sentence or two about the ones you checked. Looking over the list, Libby found herself mentally checking off characteristics for the other members of the FFW—checks beside *brilliant* and *strange* for Alex, for instance, and *beautiful* and perhaps *phony* for Wendy. She was still deciding on checks for the others when the bell rang for the end of the period.

Libby was on her way to her locker a few minutes later

when she heard hurrying footsteps behind her. A moment later Wendy caught up and fell into step. "Hi," she said. "Wasn't that the pits? Tierney's story, I mean. Like, she must have just about copied it out word-for-word." And then before Libby could answer, "I've been, like, sooo totally excited about maybe getting to see your house. Have you thought about when I could come over? Like, maybe I could ride home with you on the bus someday. You do ride the bus, don't you? I mean, I could go most anytime as long as I call my folks first. I've told them all about it. You know, about us being in this workshop together, and they think it's just so exciting that—"

It was at that moment that loud, clumping footsteps startled Wendy into silence and suddenly Tierney was walking on the other side of Libby. "Hey, Mighty Mouse," she said, "that really blew me away. About you being a thirties freak, I mean." She didn't say anything to Wendy or even look at her. "And I can't believe you really have all those Big Little Books? Man! I guess you know that for serious collectors Big Little Books are, like, what it's all about. You think I could see your collection someday?"

"Well . . ." Libby said, stalling for time while she tried to think of a good excuse. "I think that—maybe—after Easter vacation I might . . ." They'd reached the hall intersection by then, but when Libby started to turn, Tierney grabbed her wrist and jerked her around the corner. "Your locker's down by the science lab, right? I'll walk down with you."

Trotting and stumbling as she tried to keep up with her right hand, Libby could only look back briefly over her shoulder at Wendy, who was standing in the middle of the hall staring after her. She tried to wave, but her other arm was full of books. Wendy was still standing there a few seconds later when Libby flew around the next corner behind Tierney, like a puppet on a string.

10

After that day the pressure for a visit to the McCall House was really on. And not just on Wednesdays when the FFW met, either. Not now that Libby had started seeing quite a lot of Wendy and Tierney on other days of the week as well.

It started one day when Libby was arriving at school. Wendy and three of her best friends were standing in the hall not far from the front entrance, and when Libby came in, she called, "Hey, Libby. Come over here." Libby thought of pretending she hadn't heard, but in the end she decided it was obvious that she had, so she made her way, warily, across the hall through the crowd of arriving students.

Wendy's friends were wearing baggy acid-washed jeans and Reeboks and huge men's jackets and other stylish things, and they all had figures and the right kinds of hairdos. For an awful moment Libby thought Wendy might be planning to try to get an invitation for her whole gang to visit the McCall House. She didn't, though. In fact she never even mentioned the house while her friends were around. Instead she just introduced Libby to everybody. And when one of her friends, the one with frizzy blond hair and spandex pants, whispered something about McBrain, Wendy called her a dorf and asked her why she didn't just get lost.

The other girls left then, and Wendy walked with Libby clear to the door of her first-period class, and when she left, she said, "See you at lunch." But it didn't turn out that way. At lunch Tierney saw Libby first and dragged her over to where she'd been sitting with two of her friends.

Tierney didn't talk about visiting the McCall House either, at least not while her friends were there, but she did talk about her collection of stuff from before the Second World War. Her friends, a scrawny boy with almost no hair and enormous black shoes, and a tall, thin girl with tattoos and lots of earrings, didn't seem to be collectors like Tierney. But they were very interested in Libby and in the fact that Graham McCall had been her grandfather.

However, both Tierney and Wendy continued to hint about visiting the McCall House every time they had a chance to talk to Libby alone. And Libby still had good reasons not to invite them. Not the same ones she'd had at first, perhaps, but good reasons nevertheless.

Right at first she had been determined not to let any of them visit the house because she was sure they only wanted to have something new to laugh at and make fun of. They'd laugh all right, she'd been sure of that, the way they laughed and poked fun at anything and anyone who was different. And the McCall House was certainly different. The enormous old crumbling castle with its overgrown yard and dangling shutters was certainly not at all like the homes of most Morrison Middle Schoolers. And her family of four and sometimes five adults—including one nonrelated adult male and a mostly absentee actress mother—would probably seem weird to them too.

But now she wasn't so sure about their reasons for wanting to visit. She believed Wendy now when she said she'd been fascinated by the house for years because it was so outrageously mysterious and she'd always loved mysterious old houses. And she almost believed Tierney, too, when she raved about how much she wanted to see Libby's thirties collection. But there was another problem about inviting either of them.

Since the whole thing had been Wendy's idea in the first place, it wouldn't be fair to ask Tierney and not Wendy. To ask Wendy and not Tierney would probably be downright dangerous. And to ask them both at the same time would obviously be extremely uncomfortable, to say the least, considering how they felt about each other. So Libby tried to avoid talking to either of them alone, and meanwhile a couple of weeks passed and the FFW kept meeting and everyone was working on new stories and reading them in the workshop.

Alex was working on a new parody.

"It's a blast," he told Libby one Wednesday afternoon while they were waiting for the others to arrive. "I suppose you've read *Watership Down,* haven't you."

Libby nodded. Elliott had brought it home from the bookstore for her a long time ago.

"Yeah, I thought you probably would have. Well, I'm writing this parody about this noble and heroic bunch of gophers who live in a vacant lot in the city until it's paved over to make a parking lot. And then they escape to a miniature golf course and set up a great society with gopher senators and gopher poets and gopher four-star generals and like that."

Libby said she couldn't wait to hear it, and Alex grinned and said he couldn't wait to hear her next one either, and what was it about? So she told him that she'd still had more chapters of "Rainbow" to read, but that she'd started work on something new that she wasn't ready to talk about yet.

They took their seats then and got out their manuscripts. Libby noticed that Alex's looked terribly professional, as if it had been printed on a printing press instead of a typewriter. When she asked him about it, he said it was done on a word processor and that he had one of his own at home.

"Don't you have a word processor?" he asked in a surprised tone of voice.

"Me?" Libby said. "No. I started learning how to use one at Elliott's store—he's a friend of ours who lives with us. But I don't have one at home."

"You ought to get one. They're the greatest," Alex said.

"I know. But they're too expensive. We can't afford it."

Alex widened his eyes, twisted the corners of his mouth down, and wagged his head back and forth.

"What's that supposed to mean?" Libby asked, frowning.

"That," Alex said, "is supposed to be 'wild surmise.' " I'm looking at you with 'wild surmise.' "

92

Libby went on frowning for a moment—and then giggled. "What are you surmising?"

"That I must be wrong about you being a millionaire. I thought you must be one. I mean, your grandfather was famous and everything and you live in that great big rocky mountain of a house that everyone's so absolutely crazy to see."

Libby shook her head. "My grandfather was rich once. But he always spent money faster than he made it, even when he was alive and famous. And his books don't sell very well now. And my father is a poet. Poets don't make much money."

"Yeah. So I've heard. But anyway, you ought to get your own word processor as soon as you can. But at least you have a typewriter. I used to work on a typewriter. It was better than nothing, but not nearly as great as a word processor."

"Well," Libby said. "I don't really have a typewriter either. Not of my own anyway. But there's this old one that used to be my grandfather's and—"

"Wow!" Alex said, grabbing Libby's manuscript out of her hand. "You mean this was actually typed on Graham McCall's own typewriter? Wow." And then as Tierney stomped through the door, "Hey, look at this. This was actually typed on the same original typewriter that Graham McCall wrote *Milk and Honey* on. Wasn't it, Libby?"

Libby said it was, as far as she knew, but she couldn't be sure since she hadn't been around at the time. Tierney seemed to be very impressed.

"I'll bet it's a great big tall thing with keys that come up like on these big levers, like Dashiell Hammett and everybody used back in the thirties," she said. And, of course, she went on to say how much she'd like to see it, and when Wendy came in, she said she would too. They were both still looking at Libby expectantly when Mizzo came in and called the class to order.

That turned out to be the first day they worked on the joint writing project that Mizzo called "The Island Adventure." It was Mizzo's idea and when she first explained how it was going to work, no one else was very enthusiastic. She was going to start things off by reading the first episode of a story, and then everyone would take the story from there and write a short second part at home during the week. The following Wednesday Mizzo would read everyone's chapter without saying who wrote which and they would vote on which one was best. Then she would reread the winner, and during the next week they would all go on from that point in the story.

Libby thought she knew what Mizzo was trying to do. She was trying to make the members of the FFW understand and appreciate each other more by having them work on something together. Libby wasn't at all sure it was going to work. In fact she really doubted that the way Tierney and Wendy felt about each other, as well as the way Alex and G.G. felt about each other, was going to be changed that easily.

Mizzo's first "Island Adventure" described a violent storm at sea. The five members of the FFW are on a ship going to a convention of young winners of writing contests in another country, but they obviously are not going to make it. The ship is sinking. But at the last possible minute they locate a lifeboat and the five of them climb aboard and lower themselves down into the sea. After a few dangerous hours the boat washes up on the shore of an island.

Mizzo's story ended there, but there were a couple of questions before they moved on to something else. Alex wanted to know about point of view—if you had to write from your own point of view, "In my case the point of view of Alexander Lockwood, for instance, or if I can be omniscient and get inside the heads of the other four"—he looked around the room, grinning— "characters? And in this case *characters* is exactly the right word."

Then Tierney said he'd better stay out of her head if he knew what was good for him, and that she had a question, too. Tierney's question was, Would it be all right if she killed off some of the characters?

It was obvious that Mizzo was trying to keep a straight face as she said that point of view would be up to them, but she thought she'd better rule out killing off other characters or there would soon be no one left to write about. Then she went on to call on Wendy to be the first reader of the day.

Wendy's new story was about a family who had just moved to a huge old house that was supposed to be haunted. The first chapter was full of creaking doors and ghostly glowing lights, as well as quite a bit about what kind of clothes everybody was wearing and what color their eyes and hair were and who they were in love with.

During the critique the comments were better than the ones about her "pink" story. Most of the comments were favorable, except that Tierney did suggest that the title should be "The Ghosts of Sweet Valley High." But no one said anything very insulting, not even G.G.

Gary Greene, as a matter of fact, didn't seem to be

behaving normally at all. He was sitting quietly with his head down and turned away, so all Libby could see was that he was wearing dark glasses and there was what looked like a dirty spot on his left cheek.

"I liked it okay," he said when Mizzo asked him to comment on the story. "Better than that pink-dress thing, anyway." At least that was what he seemed to be saying, but his voice was so mumbly and indistinct it was hard to be sure.

Alex poked Libby and twitched his head toward G.G. "Wonder what happened to the ghoul," he whispered. "Maybe one of his victims turned out to be a karate expert."

Alex was grinning and so was Libby, but when Mizzo called on G.G. to read and he turned to face the group for the first time, their smiles faded.

"Good heavens, Gary," Mizzo gasped. "What happened?"

Both of G.G.'s lips were split and swollen and there were bruises on his jaw and darker ones that spread down his cheeks from behind the dark glasses. While everyone was staring at him in horror, he shrugged his shoulders and made a laughing noise without moving his lips. "Football game," he mumbled. "Me and two hundred pounds of high school hotshot collided. You should see the other guy."

Libby ducked her head and looked around at the others through her hair. Tierney was grinning gleefully, but all the others, Mizzo included, looked as if they were doing the same thing Libby was—which, to be specific, was that she was gloating a little because G.G. certainly deserved to get the worst of it, for once—and, at the same time, feeling guilty because what had happened to him was too terrible to wish on anyone, even Gary Greene. Of course, Mizzo had to excuse G.G. from reading, and when she asked if there were any volunteers, the only one was Alex.

So Alex read next, and everyone liked "Watertrap Down," the story of the gopher colony in the miniature golf course. They all laughed like crazy, particularly in the part where the gophers sent out a war party to raid a nearby pet store and rescue a bunch of white mice from the cruel pet store owner, who was planning to feed them to a ten-foot boa constrictor. And when the boa constrictor followed them back to their golf course, they set up a golf-ball cata-pult and bombed him with Omegas and Spalding Top-Flites until he gave up and retreated down a sewer pipe.

There was another part of the "Watertrap Down" par-ody that Libby particularly liked. Just as in the original story, one of the important episodes concerned the colony's search for some females to join their new settlement. There was a heroic march and battle to free the females and then the journey back to the golf course. And all the way back the lady gophers, who had names like Tootsie and Sweety Pie, were crying and giggling and talking baby talk and doing all kinds of stupid things.

Libby saw what Alex was doing, but some of the others didn't at first. "That stuff about getting the females was dumb, though," Tierney said during the discussion. "How come the male gophers were all so great and wise and intel-ligent, and all the females were bubble brains? You some kind of a male chauvinist, Lockwood?"

Alex bounced and twitched with excitement. "No," he almost shrieked. "You're missing the point. *I'm* not chau-vinistic. But the book is. *Watership Down* is, I mean. You read the book? The female rabbits weren't exactly mental giants, were they?"

Tierney thought for a moment, and then she began to nod her head. "Yeah," she said, "they weren't, were they? I get it." Then she grinned her evil grin at Alex and said, "So, you can stop squeaking at me, Lockwood. *I get it!*"

That afternoon, on her way home, Libby thought a lot about "Watertrap Down" and Alex Lockwood. As she walked along, she started trying to figure out what she would say if she were writing something about Alex.

He's weird, she would write. *Nervous and twitchy and almost crazy-acting sometimes. From what I hear, he has to go to special classes part of the time, as if he were retarded or something, and he told me himself that he can't write, although he must have been kidding. At the same time, HOW-EVER, he's just about the funniest, most talented person I've ever met. And the most quick-witted, too.*

That quick-witted part fascinated her almost more than anything else, because that was something she knew she wasn't. She knew she was smart. The family had always told her so, and she knew she was able to learn things that a lot of people her age couldn't—if she could do it more or less on her own and at her own rate of speed. But she had also discovered that if she were nervous or under pressure, she sometimes couldn't remember things that she knew very well, let alone making up clever and witty new things on the spur of the moment.

Alex Lockwood, she would write in her journal, *is the most quick-witted person I've ever met.* That was definitely what she would say, she decided. She would go out to the Treehouse as soon as she got home and write it in her journal—the green one with all the rest of the stuff about the meetings of the FFW.

She had just finished making that decision when she turned the corner onto Westwind, and there he was waiting for her, leaning against the McCall House front gate, wearing a baggy green jacket and his nervous, jiggly grin.

Libby's shocked surprise quickly turned into indignation. Alex Lockwood had no right to be there. Putting her hands on her hips, she frowned fiercely, but he only went on grinning and jabbering all kinds of nonsense.

"Hey," he said with a grand gesture. "It's here. The movie you've all been waiting for. *Mighty Mouse Meets the Lone Stranger*. Or how about . . . *The Strange Loner?* Hey, that's good, if I do say so myself. The strange loner. Perfect typecasting."

"How—" Libby began, and was immediately interrupted.

"No, no. Wrong part. That's Tonto's line. You're Mighty Mouse."

Libby laughed—briefly, and then frowned again. "No, I'm not," she said. "What I was going to say was, *how* did you get here?"

"By bus. Simple as anything. You just climb on number seven down by the library. But you know that, don't you?"

"Okay," she said. "But—"

"I know. I know your next question. Why? That's simple too. I wanted to see the McCall House. Wendy wants to see the McCall House. Tierney wants to see the McCall House. Everybody wants to see the McCall House. *Moi aussi.* That means me too."

Libby's frown deepened. "I know what *moi aussi* means," she said. "My grandmother teaches me French. What I want to know is why you didn't ask me if you could come?"

"That's simple too. I didn't ask because you'd just have said no. But now that I'm here—now that I've come all this way . . ." Suddenly he dropped down on one knee, clasped his hands in front of him, and twisted his narrow, bony face into a ridiculous, tragic mask. "Surely you won't send me away—all alone—out into the cold, cruel world."

Libby struggled against an urge to laugh, and another urge—to give him a good kick. She settled for kicking the air near his shinbone. "Get up, you idiot," she said, glancing up and down the street to see if anyone was watching.

"Aha! I saw it. A smile. That means you're not angry. That means you're going to invite me in. Okay. Here we go." He jumped up, picked up his book bag, and pushed open the gate. *"Après vous, mademoiselle."*

Libby was still trying to stop him, still trying to explain why he couldn't come in, when she suddenly realized that he wasn't listening at all. Standing in the middle of the path, he was staring up at the house, his face quiet and still.

"Fantastic," he said softly. "It looks just like him."

"Like who?" Libby said several times before she got his attention.

"Like Graham McCall."

101

"What does?"

"The house does. It looks like what he would build. I mean, if you've read his books, you just know that he'd build this exact kind of a house."

Libby nodded. She'd always felt something like that, almost as if the house itself, in some strange way, were her grandfather. "I know," she said, and then frowned again. "How do *you* know? You haven't read his books, have you? They're not for kids."

"Sure I've read them. Why not? You have, too, haven't you? And you're younger than I am."

"But that's different. He's not *your* grandfather."

"True," Alex said. "Very true. But then, I read quite a lot of stuff that wasn't written by my grandfather." He tipped his head back and looked up again at the high stone pillars, the overhanging balconies and turreted roof. Then he jerked his shoulders up and down several times in a stuttery shrug. "Come on. I think he's waiting for us," he said, and led the way up the front steps. Libby followed.

The entry hall alone took several minutes with Alex stopping to stare at the dusty Tiffany lamps and art nouveau statues, the dark, old oil paintings, and the hand-carved pewlike bench that circled the hall, bending to the curve of the wide staircase. Libby, still resenting his presence, said nothing at all, and Alex was silent too. Except that his darting eyes, even more jittery than usual, said things about how excited and fascinated he was. Libby led him up to the landing next and showed him Graham's portrait, and he stood there staring for so long that she finally had to nudge him in the ribs and tell him firmly to come on. He came back to life then, but before he started moving, he said that he was going to have to read all of Graham's books over again, because now that he'd seen his picture, he was sure he'd get a lot more out of them.

They went back down to the library next, and there on the couch by the fireplace were Gillian and Cordelia, reading *The New York Times*. Cordelia was wearing her gray wool flannel dress with the black braid trim, and Gillian was in her lavender jumpsuit with the wide stretch belt. They both looked up, stared in astonishment, and quickly managed welcoming smiles; Cordelia's a little stiff and uncertain, and Gillian's deeply dimpled and absolutely boiling over with curiosity.

Actually it wasn't quite as embarrassing as one might expect. After Libby managed an introduction—"Uhh. This is my grandmother, Gillian McCall, and my great-aunt, Cordelia Wembley. And this is Alex Lockwood. He's in the writers' workshop with me and . . ."—she didn't have to say anything more. At that point Alex took over and did most of the talking himself.

After he shook hands and said how honored he was to meet the family of Graham McCall, he kept right on talking, explaining how he had always wanted to see the house because he was a fan of Graham McCall's books, and so were his parents. Watching him, Libby noticed that he seemed different. Almost as if he were another person than he was at school, calmer and more relaxed.

"My folks have been dying to see this place for years," he told Gillian and Cordelia, "and so when I met Libby, I thought, here's my chance to see it first and beat them to it. Kind of get one up on my parents." He stopped and grinned, mostly at Gillian. "It's kind of good for parents to be gotten one up on now and then, don't you think? Keeps them from losing interest."

Then he complimented Gillian on her dimples—and mentioned who had obviously inherited them—and Cordelia on her dress, and before long both of them were helping Libby show him the rest of the house. The four of them went through the library and Graham's study, the great hall and dining room and then up the stairs to the billiard room and the upstairs sitting room. And all the way, even while he was climbing the stairs in his strange, awkward way, Alex chatted with Gillian and Cordelia, making them laugh and asking intelligent questions about the art and furniture and architecture, and even about Christopher and his poetry.

That really surprised Libby—that Alex knew about her father's poetry. And it was obvious that it surprised Gillian and Cordelia too. Even the most successful poets usually aren't really famous, and Christopher was probably a little less famous than most. But Alex knew quite a lot about him and his poetry, and he also seemed to be aware of other things about poets that you might not expect a Morrison Middle School student to understand. When Gillian offered to take him out to the gazebo where Christopher was working, to be introduced, he said, "Oh, no. I couldn't interrupt a poet while he's writing. That's one of the Ten Commandments, isn't it? Thou shalt not interrupt the writing of poetry." And Gillian laughed and said that he was probably right and that if it wasn't one of the Ten Commandments, it ought to be.

There were no more introductions to make, since Elliott was still at the bookstore, but the tour itself lasted a long time. Cordelia wanted to show Alex the Great Hall's over-hanging balconies, and Gillian decided he should see her dance studio with its practice bar and mirror-lined walls. Then Gillian and Cordelia went back downstairs, but before she left, Gillian told Alex about the third floor, and of course he had to see that too. Libby hadn't been planning to mention it.

The old servants' quarters on the third floor had been empty for a long time, except for Libby's collections. The first room was mostly ancient Greece with a bit of Roman Empire. The furnishings consisted of a couple of old kitchen tables and a lot of shelves that had once been in the store-room at Elliott's store. The walls were covered with pic-tures, scenes of Greece and Rome, mostly illustrations from magazines, and on the shelves and tables there were several copies of Greek statues, a model of the Parthenon, a collec-tion of old Roman coins (copies actually), and dozens of books and scrapbooks.

Alex walked around the room several times, bending forward to peer at pictures and picking things up to ex-amine them more closely. "Hey, great!" he kept saying. "Wow!" and other enthusiastic remarks. "Did you do all this? I mean, did you collect all this stuff?" he asked finally.

So Libby explained how it had begun years before when she started making collections concerning whatever she happened to be studying. It had all been in one room at first, with a wall or table for each country and subject, but then the whole family got interested, and the collections grew until they spread out over most of the third floor.

The second room, the British Empire, was furnished and decorated much the same as the first, except that an illustrated time line ran all the way around the room, marked off with dates of all the important events. The illustrations, pictures of all kinds and sizes, were arranged above and below the time line, along with paper figures depicting all the English kings and queens. From each picture or royal figure pieces of yarn led to their proper dates.

The third room was dedicated to the pioneer period. There was a longhorn-steer skull on one wall, a stuffed rattlesnake on a table, and another wall was covered by a huge map of the United States with all the famous pioneer trails drawn across it in different colors.

Alex seemed to be particularly interested in the pioneer room. "This is amazing," he said after he'd spent a lot of time staring at the rattlesnake and the miniature model of a Conestoga wagon pulled by an ox team. "Where did you get all this stuff?" So Libby explained about the attic. The Mc-Call House attic was enormous and absolutely crammed full of souvenirs that various members of the family had picked up during their travels.

"All of them used to travel a lot," she told him. "Gillian lived in France when she was studying to be a ballet dancer, and she got to go to most of the countries in Europe. And Cordelia traveled all over the world when she was married to Alfred Wembley. And Elliott has traveled a lot too. But most of the things in the attic used to be Graham's. He loved to travel, and everywhere he went, he bought all kinds of souvenirs. Gillian says that Graham tried to bring the whole world back to Morrison with him. Like, he got that rattlesnake in Arizona, and the covered wagon is from Texas. Sometimes Gillian says that one of his souvenirs was a ballet dancer, from Paris—meaning herself, of course."

Alex grinned, "Yeah," he said. "That's good. That's exactly what she looks like. Not many people have grandmothers that look like a souvenir from Paris, but you do." He went on grinning and nodding as he circled the room once more before he asked, "And all the books?"

"A lot of them are from Graham's library, but the newest ones are from Elliott's store. They all let me use things for my displays, but I have to give them back when I'm finished with the project."

"You mean you change these rooms all the time?"

Libby nodded. "Most of them. Like, this room was China last year, and the British Empire used to be Napoleon. But the Thirties Room doesn't get changed, because it's not just a study project. The thirties is more like a hobby. Come on. You might as well see it too."

The sign on the door said, You Are Now Entering the 1930s. And below the sign there was a collage of pictures of thirties scenes; original pictures painted by Libby and Gillian as well as some cut from magazines or photocopied from the pages of books—scenes from everything from a Laurel and Hardy movie to the Spanish Civil War. And when you opened the door and stepped inside, you found yourself in the past.

The room, which had been the servants' parlor, was quite large and, unlike the others, was completely furnished. There were chairs, lamps, tables, and sideboards in the sleek, streamlined thirties style, with rounded, waterfall edges. A big old hand-cranked phonograph sat in one corner and a radio in an art deco floor cabinet in another. On the walls were under-construction photos of the Empire State Building and the Golden Gate Bridge, and others of famous thirties people, like movie stars such as Humphrey Bogart and Henry Fonda, and Shirley Temple when she was a very little girl, and the five Dionne sisters, the famous little girls who were the first quintuplets to live to grow up. The shelves held old, dusty books and comic strips, and miniature cars, mostly Model T Fords and Cords and Packards, and in the cabinets were thirties-style dishes and toys, and all kinds of other artifacts.

Alex looked around the room for so long that Libby finally curled up in one of the chairs with a Big Little Book that she hadn't read for a while, *Dan Dunn and the Lost Gold Mine.* She'd finished the first chapter before he stopped looking and sat down on the couch.

"Incredible, as Mizzo would say," he said. Libby didn't say anything, and after a while he went on. "Anyway, I can see now why you're so smart. What a great way to be educated."

"It didn't seem like being educated," Libby said. "It mostly seemed like a kind of game."

"Yeah, I know," Alex said. "That's what I mean. But why the thirties? Does it have something to do with Graham McCall? I mean, because so many of his books were about the thirties? At least the most famous ones?"

Libby shrugged. "I suppose he had something to do with it. He wrote about the thirties, and he collected a lot of the things in this room. And Gillian says she thinks the people in this house are still living in the thirties." She smiled. "You know, like in the Great Depression. Gillian hates not having money. She says"—Libby imitated Gillian, rolling her eyes up and sighing dramatically— "I wasn't cut out to be poor."

108

They both laughed. Libby was thinking about what she had just done, acting something out like she always did but just for the family, when Alex pointed to the Big Little Book. "Could I see that for a minute?"

Libby handed him the book and he said, "Hey. Great. I've heard about these but I've never seen one before." He leafed through the book quickly and then began to read. Now and then he read a line out loud, chuckling to himself or grinning at Libby.

She watched him and wondered—about a lot of things. By the time he closed the book and put it down, she'd gotten up her nerve to ask the thing she wondered about most.

"Errr!" she said to get his attention, and when he looked up, she asked, "What did you mean when you said you couldn't write?"

He grinned and raised his eyebrows. "I can't. At least not so anyone can read it. That's why I'm in love with my word processor." He shrugged. "It's part of the whole problem."

"Problem?" Libby asked.

His smile went lopsided. "Don't tell me you haven't noticed? Everybody notices. What it's called medically is cerebral palsy, but I like to think of it as a kind of a dual personality. See, it's like this. I have this smooth, cool, brilliant personality that only controls what goes on inside my head, and the rest of me is under the control of this fiendish practical joker. Like, this guy really gets his kicks out of making me look ridiculous."

Libby knew something about cerebral palsy. "But I thought cerebral palsy—" she began, but Alex interrupted.

"Yeah, I know. Most people who have it are in wheel-

109

chairs or at least are a lot worse off than I am. My doctor says I'm one of the lucky ones."

He looked away, and his almost constant grin faded. He didn't seem to be actually talking to anyone when he went on. "Yeah. Real lucky. Too lucky to get much sympathy, but unlucky enough to be in for a hell of a lot of humiliation."

12

That evening, the evening of the day that Alex appeared suddenly at the front gate, Libby climbed up into the Treehouse to write. She did it the proper and approved way this time—up the circular staircase, followed by Salome and Ariel. And as soon as the three of them were settled in the main room of the Treehouse, she got out the green journal, the one she'd been using to record information about Morrison Middle School and the FFW. Her first sentence was exactly what she'd been planning before Alex made his surprise visit. Nothing that happened that afternoon at the McCall House had changed her mind in the slightest about that.

Alex Lockwood, she wrote, *is the most quick-witted person I've ever met.* But when that was written, she just sat there for a long time drumming on the tabletop and thinking about what had happened that afternoon—the things that had been said, and maybe the things that should have been said and weren't. Ariel jumped up on the table and batted at her drumming pencil, but she shoved her away and went on thinking.

I didn't know what to say, she finally wrote, *when he said that about humiliation. I just sat there staring at him in complete speechlessness. And then he started smiling again and said, "You don't know what I'm talking about, do you?" And I said yes, I did, and he said no I didn't and how could I when I'd lived in this great place all my life with all my fantastic famous relatives and never had any serious problems.*

So, at that point, I got slightly furious and I told him he didn't know what he was talking about. And he said what did I mean, and I said I had a VERY serious problem. And he grinned and said what kind of problem, like mental or physical, or what? So I said, "Well, mostly physical, I guess," and he stopped grinning and stared at me for a minute, and then he asked what was wrong with me, was I sick, or what.

So I said, "Well, it's obvious, isn't it? I'm just not right physically for middle school. You know what they call me. Things like Mighty Mouse and McBrain and Little Franken-stein."

He started grinning then and shaking his head like he was amazed about something. And then he finally said, "That is so funny," and I said, "What is?" and he didn't say anything for a while and then he said, did I know what he envied the most about me? "Guess," he said. "Guess what you have that I envy most." So I guessed maybe the McCall House or having a famous grandfather and he said no, that what it was, was something physical. "It's the way you move," he said. "I noticed it the first time I saw you. The way you

move, like all of your bones and muscles work together per-
fectly, like a dancer or a gymnast. Like this completely effi-
cient machine. Okay, small maybe, but absolutely efficient."
  So I said that was probably because I'd been taking bal-
let lessons since I was three years old. And he said that might
be part of it, but most of it is something you're born with.
And then he said, "Cerebral palsy is something you're born
with too."

It was getting late by then and it was cold in the
Treehouse, and even Ariel and Goliath had given up and
gone away, probably headed back to the warmth of the
Great Hall. So Libby made her way up the tree limb to her
room and went to bed, but there was more that she could
have written if there'd been time, and she went on thinking
about it after she was in bed.

Alex had gone on talking for quite a while. He'd talked
about knowing that he was different before he started school
—knowing vaguely but not worrying about it, because it
didn't seem all that important. But then, when he was six,
he found out. Particularly if you're a boy, he said, you find
out what it means to be the only kid in the class who can't
throw a ball or catch one, or run across the playground
without falling down. As soon as you start school, he said,
you find out who you really are in a hurry.

"You find out you're a clown," he said. "A dork, a nerd,
a spaz. Somebody who can be laughed at and pushed
around and used for a punching bag." Then he grinned.
"And that's just when you're six. By the time you're eight,
things *really* start getting unpleasant."

He laughed about it. Libby found that really intriguing.

She wondered if she would ever be able to laugh about some of the humiliating things that had happened to her at Morrison Middle School.

The next time the writers' workshop met, Libby wasn't the first one to arrive. She'd meant to be, but at the last moment she decided to go to her locker first, and it had taken longer than she'd expected. When she arrived at the reading lab, the rest of them were already there waiting.

As she opened the door, she thought she heard voices, but as soon as they saw who it was, it got suddenly quiet. Libby was hurrying to her seat when Tierney and Wendy began talking at once.

"Hey, Mighty Mouse," Tierney said. "Where you been?"

And Wendy said, "Hi, Libby. You're here after all. We thought maybe you were absent. I didn't see you in the hall this morning, and then you weren't the first one here like always. We'd about decided you were sick or something."

Safely in her seat, Libby glanced around. Everyone was smiling. Alex's grin was, as usual, crooked and jumpy, and Wendy's was the usual, too, multipurpose bright and shiny. Tierney's was something new, however, a real smile, even though it looked a little bit painful, as if her face wasn't used to it. But G.G.'s was the same as always—a dangerous leer.

"I told you she was here," G.G. said. "I saw her in math class—just like always." He mugged a frightened expression, and tipping his binder up on end, he ducked his head down behind it.

They all looked at him—but nobody laughed. At least not until Tierney said, "Aww, poor baby. You don't have to do that anymore, G.G. Your face is almost back to normal."

Mizzo came in then, and the workshop started. The first thing she did was collect the new installments of "The Island Adventure" and read them out loud. It was pretty easy to tell who had written each one, particularly the one about a bloody war with a fierce tribe of headhunters who lived on the island, and another about meeting a handsome and muscular jungle boy and falling in love with him. But the version that won in the voting was about how all five members of the group struggled through high winds and tidal waves to find a cave in a hillside, where they built a kind of fortress. It was told in short, clear sentences and was extremely tense and exciting—even though some of it did sound a little bit like *Robinson Crusoe*.

It turned out to be Tierney's, and she really looked pleased when she found out that she had won, and when Mizzo asked her to be the first reader of the day, she didn't argue. She got out her manuscript quickly, and before she began to read, she looked around at everybody with what was definitely a "wait-till-you-hear-this expression" on her face.

As soon as she started reading, it was obvious that she had written another mystery, but this time it wasn't of the Sam Spade/Philip Marlowe variety. The new mystery, which was called "The Case of the Purple Parrot," was set in a town that seemed to be very similar to Morrison, instead of in Los Angeles, and the detective was a teenage girl.

The girl in the story, whose name was Jade, was sixteen years old, but she lived all by herself in a luxurious apartment and drove a silver Ferrari. She was extremely beautiful and intelligent and courageous, and she solved a mystery about a murder that happened in a pet shop near where she lived. It turned out that the pet shop owner had been selling drugs, and the girl detective broke up a drug ring and solved a crime that had been baffling the police and the FBI for months.

It was a long story, and reading it took a lot longer than the usual time limit, but every time Mizzo started to interrupt, Tierney just glared at her and read faster. When the mystery was finally solved and the story ended, she folded the manuscript, lifted her chin, and looked around the room with a triumphant frown, as if she were daring anyone to say anything critical.

Wendy began, and with a self-righteous expression on her face like someone saying the right thing even if it killed her, she said she liked the main character and that she thought the story was exciting. G.G. was next and he said he liked it, too, except for the murder itself, which should have been the best part but instead was kind of vague and uninteresting.

When it was Libby's turn, she pointed out that the story was well plotted, so that there were some early clues that helped the readers solve the mystery if they were paying attention, which is very important in mystery writing. But then she asked Tierney how it happened that Jade lived all by herself if she was only sixteen and how she got the Ferrari and everything. And Tierney said it was because she was an orphan, a rich orphan, whose parents had died and left her gobs of money. So Libby suggested that maybe that should have been explained in the story to make it seem a little more realistic, because it really was a pretty unusual situation. She got a little carried away, in fact, and said more than she meant to, but Tierney didn't seem to get too angry.

When Mizzo asked Alex to comment, he went into a kind of nervous fit, twisting his head and grinning and rolling his eyes around. Libby turned her eyes away, knowing he didn't have to act that way and wishing he wouldn't. At last he got a sheepish expression on his face and said, "Now, look, Tierney. I don't want to make you mad or anything, but I just want to say that I think you've written another really great parody. I mean, what I think is that you just have a natural talent for writing really neat parodies, and that's a compliment and—"

Wendy suddenly bounced in her seat and raised her hand. "Yes," she said without waiting to be called on, "it is. It is, Mizzo, isn't it? It's a parody, like of Nancy Drew, isn't it?"

But Tierney ignored Wendy and went on glaring at Alex. "Now *you* look, Lockwood," she practically shouted. "This is not a parody, and if you don't shut up about your stupid parodies, I'm going to parody you one, right in the nose."

Everybody laughed, especially Alex.

There wasn't much time left, but it was G.G.'s turn next, and Mizzo asked him if he'd like to read some of what he'd been working on.

"Me?" he said. "My turn?" He started to open his binder and then quickly closed it and put both hands on it as if he were holding it shut. "No," he said. "I didn't write any more. I've had too much other stuff to do lately."

117

"But how about what you were working on in class yesterday?" Mizzo said. "It looked to me as if you'd written quite a lot."

"Oh, that," G.G. said. "Well . . ." He stared down at his binder for a moment and then opened it slowly and looked at the first page. He looked at it for quite a while before he began to read.

" 'Eric,' " he read. "That's the title. See, that's this guy in the story's name. I haven't thought up any other title yet. Okay?

" 'ERIC'

"Eric got home from school late that day because his bicycle had a flat and he spent a long time trying to get it fixed, and finally he had to give up and walk it home. When he got to the house, he put the bike in the garage and went in the back door. The house was empty as usual, but there was a note on the kitchen sink. He read the note quickly and then looked at the clock on the stove. He was late. He couldn't do what the note told him to do because it was too late.

"He stared at the clock for a minute and then he ran into the living room to check the clock on the desk, because it didn't seem possible it could be that late. But the desk clock said the same thing.

"There wasn't anything he could do about it, so he just went ahead and fixed himself some leftover spaghetti in the microwave and went into the living room to watch the tube while he ate. When he was finished, he went back to the kitchen and read the note again. But it was still too late, and there still wasn't anything he could do about it."

The story went on telling how Eric watched television some more and then went to bed and waited. It didn't say what he was waiting for, but just that he waited and listened and told himself that there was no use worrying because there wasn't anything he could do about it and whatever was going to happen would just have to happen. While he was waiting, he heard noises in the house that turned out to be the refrigerator or the furnace, and noises outside the house that came from cars and the neighbors having a party.

As G.G. read, his voice got softer and higher pitched, so you had to listen carefully to tell what he was saying. The last sentence he read was, "It was nearly one o'clock in the morning when he heard the sound he'd been expecting. Exactly what he'd been expecting." Then he suddenly slammed the binder shut, and said, "That's it. That's as far as I got."

Libby caught her breath. It was as if she'd been listening so hard she'd almost forgotten to breathe. She felt drained and blank with listening. The others were blank-faced, too —no smiles or grins or frowns. Libby tried to think why. The story was short and nothing much happened, unlike G.G.'s other stories, where everything happened in horrible detail.

Mizzo was just starting to ask for comments when the bell rang for the end of class.

13

A few minutes later that same afternoon Libby was at her locker getting the books she needed to take home when right behind her a startlingly loud voice said, "Hey, Mighty Mouse. You going home now?" Of course it was Tierney.

Since the last class of the day had just ended, the answer to Tierney's question was pretty obvious. It did occur to Libby to say that, no, she was actually just arriving early for Thursday morning. She didn't say it, but she was pleased she'd thought of it. What she did say was, "Yes, I guess so. Aren't you?"

"Sure," Tierney said. "At three-twenty I'm outta here. Come on. Let's split. I want to talk to you."

Libby knew what was coming, or at least she thought she did. Tierney was about to make another pitch for a visit to the McCall House. This time, however, it turned out to be something different, or perhaps a slightly less direct approach to the same thing. What Tierney had in mind was that Libby should come home with her to see the stuff she'd collected and just to "hang out for a while."

At first Libby tried to think of a good excuse not to go. But then, while she was still trying to decide which excuse sounded most convincing, she suddenly realized that she didn't particularly want to get out of going. She was, in fact, a little bit intrigued, not only with the idea of seeing what kind of a collection Tierney had but even more so with finding out where she lived and perhaps some information about the home environment of a person with pink hair.

"Okay," she said. "But I can't stay very long unless I call home and let them know where I am."

"Sure," Tierney said, and then, in a high, squeaky alien-type voice, "Mighty Mouse call home. If E.T. can call home, why not Mighty Mouse. What planet are you from, anyway? If it's the same one as E.T., all we need is a few clothes hangers and an old record player. Right?"

And Libby said, "Right!" even though she had never seen *E.T.* and didn't really know what Tierney was talking about.

Tierney lived on Balsam Avenue, only a few blocks from the school but on the other side of Main Street. On the way through the downtown section they stopped once or twice to look in shop windows—a pet shop first and then a Gap outlet that had some new baggy-looking denim jackets in the window.

While they were looking in the pet shop window at some guinea pigs and white mice, Libby started grinning, and she noticed that Tierney was doing the same thing.

"Yeah," Tierney said. "The gopher thing. I was thinking about the same thing. That was really rad. I mean that

121

Lockwood character is really a rad writer. Too bad he's such a nerd."

"Nerd?" Libby asked.

"Yeah. Squirmy. Jumpy. You know. The square root of uncool." She hitched up one shoulder and did a nervous tic thing with one side of her face.

"Yes," Libby said. "Well, he has cerebral palsy, for one thing."

Tierney stopped grinning. "Yeah? Is he going to die, or what?"

Libby shook her head. "You don't die of cerebral palsy. It doesn't get worse or anything. It's just something you're born with and it doesn't go away."

Tierney went back to looking in the window. After a while she said, "Hey. Look at that guinea pig. The Blob—with fur."

They'd walked on down the street for about half a block before she said, "Hey, I didn't know that—about Lockwood, I mean. You should have told me before."

The next time they stopped, to look at the denims in The Gap, they were standing in the sunshine, and the shop window was almost like a mirror. They looked at their reflections for a minute, and then they looked at each other and grinned.

"Hey, Mighty Mouse," Tierney said. "Would you mind walking on the other side of the street? People are going to think I play with kindergartners."

"Yes," Libby said. "Or else they'll think I'm with my mother."

Tierney pretended to hit her and then they both convulsed with laughter. What made it so funny was that, no matter how big she was, Tierney—with her spiky pink hair and safety-pin earrings—certainly didn't look like anybody's idea of a mother. They laughed, and stopped, and looked at each other in the window and laughed again. It took several minutes for them to sober up enough to start off again down the sidewalk.

Libby wasn't familiar with the Balsam Avenue area where Tierney lived, since it was on the other side of town from the McCall House. The homes on Balsam were fairly new and quite large, and Tierney's house was one of the largest. Low and rambling with diamond-paned windows and a steep shake roof, it would have looked like a country cottage if it hadn't been so big—as if someone had been trying to build the largest country cottage in the whole world.

"Well, here we are in the land of Oz. Cute, isn't it," Tierney said as she took out a key and unlocked the front door. "You better brace yourself."

"Brace myself?" Libby asked. "What for?"

"For my gorgeous family. For my totally overwhelmingly gorgeous family." The sneer was suddenly back in Tierney's voice, and when Libby checked, she could see it on her face too. What Tierney was saying about her family was obviously ironical and probably sarcastic too. As the two of them walked down the hallway toward the sound of voices at the rear of the house, Libby tried to brace herself. She didn't have any idea what to expect, but the picture in her mind was of some other very large people with crazy hairdos and weird clothing.

They found Tierney's family, at least two members of it, in the kitchen, and the amazing thing was—they really were gorgeous. Tierney's sister, whose name was Courtney and who was a senior in high school, was tall like Tierney, but very slender. She had sleek, heavy dark hair, a fashion-model figure, and a long, lovely face. Her mouth was as big as Tierney's, but somehow in Courtney's face it looked as if it were meant to be that way, instead of the result of an accident. And Mrs. Tierney looked very much like Court-ney only slightly older. They really were fantastic-looking, both of them—and they were also polite and friendly, even though Tierney wasn't.

In fact Tierney just stomped through the room without saying anything, and when her mother asked her to intro-duce her friend, she just said, "Mighty Mouse. Her name is Mighty Mouse," without pulling her head out of the refrig-erator.

Libby said hello and was starting to explain that Mighty Mouse was only a nickname, when Tierney came out of the refrigerator with two cans of 7-Up, shoved one of the cans into her hand, and started dragging her out of the room. They had already started down the hall when Mrs. Laurent called to ask if they'd like some cookies, and Tierney went back to get some, leaving Libby alone in the hallway. She couldn't quite hear what Mrs. Laurent was saying to Tier-ney in the kitchen, but she heard Tierney's answer clearly.

"Well, you didn't have to stare at her," she said. "And besides, she's a lot bigger than she looks."

Libby couldn't help giggling—even though she was still feeling embarrassed over the way Tierney had acted in the kitchen. She wanted to know how on earth a person could be a lot bigger than she looked, but when Tierney came stomping back down the hall, scowling fiercely and muttering something under her breath, she decided not to ask. By the time they got to her room the frown was completely gone.

"Here we are," she said as she threw the door open. "Step out of the time capsule, ladies and gentlemen, and into the past."

It was a large room, and they were in it for several minutes before Libby realized that it was actually Tierney's bedroom. For one thing there were so many other pieces of furniture in it—all kinds of tables, cabinets, shelves, and display cases. And for another the bed itself was almost invisible, buried under a huge pile of debris. Besides a general scattering of clothing, shoes, books, and magazines, there was the collection—Tierney's "old stuff" collection that not only packed every cabinet and display case but also spread out over every other flat surface in the room.

There were dishes, and figurines and toys, including a Shirley Temple doll and a full set of Dionne-quintuplet dolls. There were early types of telephones and toasters and radios, and even a model of Amelia Earhart's airplane. The walls were covered with posters of old movies and stage plays, and opposite the bed was a large TV set with a VCR and a whole shelf of videotapes of old movies—a lot of Marx brothers, Charlie Chaplin, and Laurel and Hardy, and even *Snow White and the Seven Dwarfs* and *Gone With the Wind.*

"You want to borrow some of the videotapes?" Tierney asked.

"Well, I'm afraid it wouldn't do me much good. We don't have a VCR."

"Oh, yeah? Well I guess you'll just have to come back

125

here sometime for a thirties retrospective. A whole lot of my movies are from the thirties. Not all of them, but a lot. We can watch old movies and eat popcorn, and I'll even give away a door prize like they used to do back in those days. Here, sit down. And that telephone works if you have to"— Tierney changed her voice to high-pitched Alienese—"call home."

The phone did work, even though it was a real antique with the mouthpiece at the top of a long stem and a bell-shaped receiver hanging down just below it. Actually Libby knew it wouldn't be necessary to phone home if she left fairly soon. By taking the bus instead of making her usual leisurely stroll, she could still be home before anyone would start worrying. But she called anyhow because she wanted to see what it would be like to use the old phone. Gillian answered, and after Libby told her she might be a little late, and put off her curious questions, she went back to exploring Tierney's room.

The collection was really fantastic. Tierney had a great many rare things—all kinds of objects that Libby had seen in antique and collectors' books and wished that she could buy.

"Where did you get these? Did they belong to your grandmother?" she asked when she was examining the Dionne-quintuplet dolls, with their frilly dresses in different shades of pastel and little golden name pins that told which doll represented which quintuplet. She was really feeling envious, because dolls were in short supply in Libby's collection. They were one thing that Graham apparently never thought of collecting back in the thirties, when he was buying nearly everything else in sight.

126

"No," Tierney said. "My dad bought them for me in an antique store in Boston when he was back there on business." And as Libby went on asking, she found that most of the other things in the room had been purchased for Tierney by various members of her family. It was very obvious to Libby, who for years had been avidly scanning the collectors' books and magazines in Elliott's store, that a great deal of money had been spent. She decided to mention the fact to Tierney.

She had stopped circling the room by then and was sitting in a chair that Tierney had cleared for her by dumping a stack of towels and clothing off onto the floor. She was examining one of the Shirley Temple dolls. The doll still had its original dress and curly blond wig.

"These are very expensive now," she told Tierney. "Your parents really have spent a lot of money on your collection, haven't they?"

Tierney shrugged. "Yeah, I guess so. They spend a lot of money on me. Trying to prove something, I guess."

"What are they trying to prove?" Libby asked.

Tierney threw herself down across her bed, sending shoes and books and even a couple of dirty dishes bouncing off onto the floor. "Who knows?" she said. She lay on her back staring at the ceiling for a while before she said, "What are they trying to prove? Well, let's see. Maybe it's that they're not sorry I was born."

Libby got up and put the Shirley Temple doll back on the shelf and then slowly picked her way back across the floor. While she stepped carefully over and around shoes, wadded-up newspapers, books, clothing, and an occasional valuable collectors' item, she was thinking about what Tierney had said, and once back in the armchair, she went on thinking about it and dealing with a confusion of thoughts and feelings.

Part of it was something she never in the world would have expected to feel, and that was a little bit sorry for Tierney. But more than sorry—a great deal more—she was feeling curious, which she wasn't exactly proud of under the circumstances, but maybe she couldn't help herself. After all, she was a writer and, according to Gillian, all real writers, as well as some ballet dancers, have a God-given talent for curiosity.

The curiosity was winning out, and she was just trying to decide on the best question to start with, when Tierney began to answer without being asked.

Still lying on her back with one arm across her eyes, she began to talk in a tense, angry voice. "Like I said, they're gorgeous. You saw my mom and Courtney. You didn't see Heather, she's away at college now, but she's the most gorgeous of all. My dad isn't, but then you don't have to be if you're a man. What my dad is, is gigantic, and kind of clunky-looking. But, like I say, that's okay, for him. And see, they had these two beautiful daughters, but my dad still wanted a big clunky boy like him, so they decided to have another kid, and what did they get? Yours truly, a gigantic, clunky girl. See, my dad is a big important lawyer and my mom has her own business, and it's like I'm their only failure. Soo—" Tierney waved her other arm in a gesture that included the whole room and everything in it. "Sooo—they have to work real hard at pretending they're not sorry."

Libby on Wednesday

That night Libby got into bed with her green journal and Graham's safari writing kit—a little lap-top desk made of wood and leather that opened out from a small, flat suitcase. After she'd pulled the covers up around her, she set up the desk and began to write—and went on writing for a long time. Most of what she wrote was about Tierney Laurent. She even started a limerick. The first two lines went:

TIERNEY LAURENT.

She is big, she is brave, she has money,
And sometimes she's terribly funny,
But . . .

She had trouble with the rest of it. She had written and then scratched out several lines ending with *mad* and *sad* before she finally fell asleep.

Sometime during the next few days Libby made up her mind. She was going to ask Tierney to visit the McCall House. And that meant it would only be fair to ask Wendy too. Having them visit together might not be very pleasant, considering the fact that they obviously hated each other, but it would certainly be the only fair thing to do.

The next consideration was, should she ask them ahead of time or wait and spring it on them at the last moment. The advantage of waiting until the day of the visit would be that perhaps one or the other of them wouldn't be able to do it on such short notice. If that happened, they couldn't be angry at her, since it wouldn't be her fault that they couldn't make it.

After giving it some careful thought, and writing down the pros and cons in her journal, she decided the "last moment" approach was the best and safest. Right after the next workshop she would ask them both to go home with her that same afternoon.

On the next Wednesday she began her preparations at

breakfast by asking the family if it would be all right if she brought a friend home with her that afternoon. Everyone seemed pleased, especially Gillian and Cordelia, who immediately wanted to know if it would be that absolutely charming Alexander boy. Libby said no, it would be a girl this time, and when Cordelia asked her name, she said, "Tierney—or else Wendy."

Cordelia looked worried. "You're planning to ask someone to come home with you whose name you don't even know?"

Libby's mouth was full of toast at the moment, and before she could answer, Gillian said, "I'm sure that's not it, Cordelia. It's just that she hasn't decided which one of her friends she is going to ask. Isn't that it, Libby?"

"Well, that's not what she said," Cordelia said. "One should be careful to say what one means, clearly and precisely."

"That's exactly what she did," Gillian said. "She said quite clearly that she was going to ask either Tierney or Wendy to come home with her. I didn't find it a bit confusing."

"Well, I certainly did and I, for one . . ."

Both Elliott and Christopher looked at Libby and grinned, and Libby grinned back, got up, and carried her dishes out to the kitchen, without either Cordelia or Gillian noticing she had gone. She had poured herself a second helping of orange juice and was drinking it when Christopher came in.

They looked at each other, and almost in unison they said, *"How many angels?"* which was part of a private joke that had begun when Christopher had told her about how supposedly sensible people had once argued violently about how many angels could dance on the point of a needle—and Libby had said they'd better not mention the subject to Gillian and Cordelia.

Of course, Libby hadn't asked for permission to bring both Tierney and Wendy, because by then she'd convinced herself that it would be highly unlikely they'd both be able to come. After all, they both had other friends they might be planning to meet, as well as things like orthodontist appointments and afterschool lessons. And as for what might happen if they both did come—Libby preferred not to think about it.

But regardless of what she might have preferred, she did find herself worrying about it from time to time, and all during the workshop it was right there like an uncomfortable itch at the back of her mind.

Mizzo started the meeting off by reading "The Island Adventure" episodes that had been written during the last week. The one that won was about how some bloodthirsty pirates landed on the island and how the Incredible Five (the FFW members) scared the pirates away by rigging up a dancing skeleton from some old bones they'd found in a cave. The story happened to be Libby's. It was the first time her "Island Adventure" chapter had won, but even during the reading and voting and winning, she was still vaguely aware of the itchy images of what it would be like to spend the afternoon with two people who felt the way Tierney and Wendy did about each other.

Except for that nagging worry it was a good session for Libby. She was beginning to read a new story that day, called "The Pierce Arrow Palace." It was set in the thirties, and she had written it over a year ago and just recently decided to rewrite it a bit and read it in the workshop. It was about a girl from a farm-worker family during the Depression, who built herself a secret hideout in the body of an abandoned car. She'd only finished a couple of pages but the critique was mostly very good, except for G.G., who said it was boring to have the old tramp turn out to be a nice guy instead of something interesting like a psychopathic killer.

Wendy read next, a short excerpt from her new story, another one about a mysterious old mansion. It occurred to Libby to wonder if she had some kind of fixation on big old houses, or if she was just trying to drop some more hints about wanted to visit the McCall House. But it was a good story, pretty scary in places, and the main characters actually had some problems that didn't have anything to do with clothes or boyfriends. Everyone seemed to like it quite a bit except Tierney, who said some rather sneaky things about how much Wendy's writing had improved and managed to make it sound like what she meant was that "it had to get better, since there wasn't any way it could have gotten worse."

After that Mizzo gave a little pep talk about how IN-CREDIBLE they all were and how much they had improved since the workshop started, and then dismissed the meeting. Libby waited until Wendy had gone out the door. Then she took a deep breath, went over to where Tierney was still slouched in her chair, and asked if she wanted to visit the McCall House that afternoon.

"What?" Tierney said, lurching to her feet so fast she almost knocked the chair over. "Are you kidding? Let's go." Grinning a wraparound grin, she started gathering up her books, but when Libby mentioned that she was going to ask Wendy, too, the smile immediately inverted itself into a fierce frown. Pulling down the corners of her mouth and making her eyebrows almost meet in the middle, she said, "What do you want to ask that wind-up Barbie doll for? She doesn't know anything about thirties stuff. Hey, come back here."

But Libby had already ducked out the door after Wendy. Catching up with her halfway down the hall, she asked her the same question. "Could you come to see the house today? You know, the McCall House. Tierney's coming, and I thought maybe you could come too."

"Today?" Wendy said. "You mean like this afternoon? Like, right this minute?"

Wendy seemed more surprised, stunned even, than pleased, and for a minute Libby thought her plan was working and that Wendy was about to say she couldn't make it. But then the strangely blank expression evolved into the familiar TV-hostess smile. "Hey, great!" she said, "Awesome! Just wait five minutes while I go call my mother. Okay?"

Trying to keep a desperate "what do I do now" feeling from showing on her face, Libby agreed to meet on the front steps in five minutes. Then Wendy raced off toward the pay phones, and Libby went back to the reading lab. Tierney was still standing in the same spot and scowling the same scowl.

"Is Miss Congeniality going?" she said.

Libby nodded warily.

"Well, then I'm *not.*"

"Well, I'm sorry," Libby said, hoping she sounded as if

134

she meant it, and she was sorry in a way. She had really wanted to show Tierney her thirties collection. But, on the other hand, it was a great relief. She told Tierney she would ask her again, maybe next week, and was halfway out the door when something grabbed the back of her coat and almost yanked her off her feet.

"Wait up," Tierney said with her evilest grin. "You don't think I'd let you go off alone with that dorf, do you? Without me along to protect you, you'd probably catch a fatal case of brain rot. Here, give me those." She grabbed some of Libby's books and put them on her own binder. "I'll carry these. No wonder you're such a midget, carrying all that heavy stuff around all the time."

Wendy was waiting on the front steps, and they started off toward the bus stop with Libby in the middle. For quite a while they all three looked straight ahead and no one said anything at all. Tierney was stomping even more than usual, and Wendy was making a humming noise that was probably meant to sound relaxed and casual but actually was more like the sizzle just before something explodes. Libby found she was breathing with difficulty, as if the air were thick and heavy with tension.

Finally Tierney said, "Hey, Mighty Mouse. What movies do you want to see when you come over again?" and Libby said she didn't care except she really liked Laurel and Hardy.

While Tierney and Libby were talking movies, Wendy looked the other way as though she didn't even hear them, but as soon as they stopped, she started in about how some of her friends were talking about Libby the other day and saying that she was really cute and in a year or two she was going to be a real killer. But she had to keep talking louder and louder because Tierney had begun to sing at the top of her lungs.

Tierney was singing "Happy Days Are Here Again," and as soon as Wendy stopped talking, Tierney stopped singing and asked Libby if she had that song in her thirties record collection.

Then they all went back to marching in silence and Libby went on feeling more and more tense and nervous. But then, without any warning at all, the tension built up until something snapped, and an entirely different emotion suddenly took over. Stopping dead in her tracks, she stomped her foot and yelled, "All right!" And when they both turned around to stare at her, she went on yelling.

"This is ridiculous," she shouted. "You're both being ridiculous. If you don't stop it right now, you're both uninvited and I'll never ask either one of you to come home with me again, and I don't care if you never speak to me again because I'm not going to speak to either of you again. Not ever!"

Her anger evaporated then—instantly—as if the yelling had pulled a cork and let it escape, and she was about to turn around and run when Tierney grinned at Wendy and said, "Well, would you look at that! A mouse tantrum. A genuine mouse tantrum right here before our very eyes. I'm pretty scared. Aren't you?"

And Wendy laughed and said to Libby—and to Tierney — "She's right, too. We were being ridiculous. I mean, like, really infantile. Right?"

And Tierney said, "Right! Agreed! Truce? Okay?"

And Wendy said, "Okay, truce." And just then the bus

went past them and they all ran the rest of the way to the bus stop and scrambled on and went bumping and giggling down the aisle and squeezed into a backseat together. All three of them.

During the bus ride they both started asking Libby questions about the McCall House, like when it was built and whether she could remember her famous grandfather and if she was born right there in the house.

So she told them that her parents had been living in New York when she was born, and no, she couldn't remember Graham McCall. "My grandfather had just died and I was only a year old when my parents came here to live," she said. And then, because she knew it was going to come up soon anyway, she went on, "And then when I was three, my mother went back to live in New York."

Wendy shrugged. "Half the people I know have divorced parents." And Tierney said, "Yeah. Me too. It's like nowadays you're practically underprivileged if you only have two parents instead of four."

"But my parents aren't divorced," Libby said. "It's just that my mother is an actress, a stage actress, and she can't live anyplace except New York."

That really interested them both. Wendy was excited about Mercedes being an actress, even when Libby told her that she was more of a character actress and usually didn't have starring roles. And Tierney said it was really rad that her mother could live where she needed to for her own career instead of following her husband around like some kind of personal slave, like most women had to. By the time that conversation was over, they'd reached Westwind Avenue and the McCall House.

137

———

That night in bed Libby wrote about the visit in her new journal.

They liked everything, she wrote, *even Cordelia.* Then she put down the pencil and leaned back on the pillows, remembering and smiling. Tierney had acted almost as excited about the house as Wendy did, and if they noticed that it was a little—well, more than a little—shabby and run-down, they didn't mention it. And they were absolutely fascinated by the thirties collection. By all the collections, really, but particularly the thirties. Wendy had been so intrigued that she'd asked Libby and Tierney if they'd help her get started on a thirties collection of her own. And they'd both been super nice to the family. Afterward Gillian and Cordelia said they were both charming and asked them to come again. And the surprising thing was that Christopher did, too, because he usually wasn't all that thrilled about meeting new people.

Libby sighed and smiled again, and picked up her pencil.

AND, she wrote, *I decided to show them the Treehouse.* She hadn't meant to. If someone had told her a few weeks ago, or even a few days ago, that she would ever show the Treehouse to anyone else, especially to anyone from Morrison Middle School, she would have said they were out of their minds. The Treehouse had always been hers alone, that is, after it stopped being Christopher's, and it had always been personal and private and secret. She didn't know why she had decided to do it. But somehow, just as they were almost ready to go home, she had suddenly said, "There's one more thing I want to show you." And she did.

Picking up her pencil she wrote, *Wendy said that she'd rather have my Treehouse than a mansion and a limousine and a whole closetful of Liz Claiborne clothes, and then Tierney said that if she could take the tree and everything that was in it back to her own backyard, she'd be willing to trade her whole collection for it. In fact, after they left, I went back out to the Treehouse to look at it again.*

Of course the Treehouse has always been very important to me, but I'm so used to having it that a lot of the time I don't think much about it. So I climbed up again and sat in the big room and imagined I was Tierney or Wendy, and then I went on up to the triangle room and sat there for a while, watching the birds and squirrels eating in the feeders outside the windows. And then I went up to the lookout tower again to kind of reexperience that too. It was interesting seeing it, like from someone else's eyes. And I saw what they meant. It really is a pretty awesome place.

Libby went on writing for quite a while that night, but after the part about the Treehouse, what she wrote wasn't so much about what happened that day as it was about Wendy and Tierney in general. She started a new page and gave it a title, "Opposites." She began by listing all the ways in which the two of them were completely different—in looks (which included clothes and makeup), and in other ways, including attitudes, behavior, and most interests. About the only thing she could think of that they were both interested in was writing, and even that hardly counted because what they wrote was so entirely different.

The last line she wrote was, *It's no wonder they hate each other.*

After that she doodled on the margin of the paper, drawing a cartoon Wendy (with long, wavy hair and lots of curves) going up one side of the paper and one of Tierney (large and clunky with spiky hair) going up the other. Then she began to think about the way they'd said good-bye to her on the front steps of the McCall House and gone off up the street together talking in excited voices. She had stayed there listening, catching bits and pieces of comments about the collections and the Treehouse, until after they reached the gate and started down the sidewalk.

She drew them again then, at the top of the paper, this time walking along side-by-side, with their mouths open and big balloons over their heads filled with lots of squiggly words. After she'd finished that drawing, she changed the last sentence to read, *It's no wonder they hated each other.*

15

Changing *hate* to *hated* turned out to be an accurate prediction, or at least things seemed to be moving in that general direction. It was on the very next day that Libby noticed Wendy and Tierney saying "Hi" to each other in front of the school and even stopping to talk for a minute.

And a day or so later, when Tierney and Libby were having lunch together in the cafeteria, Wendy came by carrying her tray—and stopped. She didn't sit down, but she stayed for a few minutes talking excitedly about *her* thirties collection—well, actually more of a twenties collection—which was already getting off to a great start.

"It just happened that way," she said. "Like, I found out we have all this really rad stuff from the twenties that used to belong to my grandmother, and I started thinking that Libby probably has just about, like, you know, already collected all the really good thirties stuff, and so I started thinking about the twenties, and reading up about it in the encyclopedia, and I found out that the twenties were really, like, pretty awesome, too. You know, like about the flappers and flaming youth and dancing the Charleston, and the Great Market Crash with all the people jumping out of skyscrapers and all that. And I've already found some pictures of flappers and this neat brass lamp, and my mom got this killer dress out of an old trunk that used to be my grandmother's. It's, like, a real authentic flapper outfit. You know, real short with this low waistline and then a fringe around the bottom."

Wendy had to put her tray down so she could use her hands to show where the dress's neckline and waistline were and make fluttering, fringy motions with her fingers just above her knees. But then, just when she seemed about to sit down in front of her tray, one of her friends yelled at her to come on or they'd stop saving her place—and she picked up her tray and went off. After she left, Tierney grinned at Libby and said, "Wouldn't you know it?"

And Libby said, "Know what?" although she pretty much knew what Tierney meant.

"The dress bit," Tierney said. And then using a bubbly, Wendyish way of talking, "Like, you know, wouldn't you like to see my really rad collection of nineteen-twenties fashions?" But somehow the way Tierney said it and grinned afterward was a lot less nasty than it used to be when the subject was Wendy Davis.

And then, on the very next day, which happened to be warm and sunny, Libby and Tierney went out to sit on the grass in the north patio after they'd finished eating lunch. Wendy was already there with a big group of her friends, but when she saw Tierney and Libby, she waved, and a few minutes later she got up and came over and sat down with them and started talking about the writing group.

First she asked Tierney what she was working on and Tierney told her, and then they all started talking about Alex and how they couldn't wait to hear what he was going to do next. Then Libby brought up something that had been stuck in her mind lately, like a lump of something in your throat that won't go down when you swallow—and that was the strange story that G.G. had started reading and then stopped.

"It's funny, but I just can't stop thinking about it," she said, and Wendy and Tierney said they'd been doing the same thing and wondering why G.G. had refused to read any more of it. Mizzo seemed to think he'd written a lot more, and he didn't deny it either. He just kept saying he wasn't ready to read it.

"Yeah," Tierney said. "There's something real weird about that. It was entirely different than his usual junk. I mean, you didn't know where it was going, or anything, but you sure wanted to find out."

"I know. I know!" Wendy said. "It really made, like, the hair stand up on the back of your neck. Didn't it?" And both Tierney and Libby agreed that it did.

That night Wendy called Libby up to talk some more about G.G.'s story, and Alex and various other topics. And from then on she called almost every evening, and soon afterward Libby started stopping off at Wendy's house now and then on her way home from school.

Unlike the Laurent family, who were, as Tierney said, overwhelmingly gorgeous, the Davis family seemed to be overwhelmingly average. Their house was only medium-sized, Wendy's two little brothers were ordinary seven- and five-year-old boys, and Mrs. Davis certainly looked and acted like an absolutely average housewife—a little bit over-weight and not at all glamorous. Mrs. Davis talked about recipes and needlework, and Mr. Davis talked about business and bowling, and the two little brothers hardly ever mentioned anything except cars and trucks.

Trying to describe Wendy's family in her journal, Libby found it hard to select many adjectives. None of the ones from Mizzo's character sketches seemed to fit—certainly none of the negative ones like *cruel, angry,* or *aggressive* and, on the other hand, none of the really positive ones like *elegant, impressive,* or *witty.* In fact the only adjective that seemed to fit the Davis family was one that Mizzo hated because it was so boring. *Nice* is a boring word, Mizzo always said—but where the Davis family was concerned, *nice* was just about as good as it got. Except, of course, for Wendy, herself, who was—whatever else she really was, besides beautiful and self-confident and poised. Libby was still trying to decide what Wendy Davis really was.

By that time, early in April, the writers' workshop had become one of the things Libby thought about on purpose when she couldn't sleep at night. But that was only the workshop. The rest of the week at Morrison Middle School hadn't changed all that much. Especially in math class, where G.G., who pretty much left Libby alone in Mizzo's workshop, still gave her lots of attention—as one of his favorite victims. But not the only one. There were six or seven other people in the room that G.G. liked to pick on. Sometimes Libby wondered about the others.

Most of them were shy, quiet people, who just suffered in silence the way Libby did when G.G. went after them. But one was a kid who had a very quick temper and who yelled and swore when G.G. baited him and sometimes got sent to the office while G.G. managed not to be blamed. But two others, a boy named Tyler and a girl named Dawn, were part of the in-group, and they were both very confident and self-assured and funny. When G.G. started running them down, they gave him back as good as they got.

"Hey, look who's stylin' now," G.G. said once when Tyler came in wearing a new bright-colored shirt. And then something like, "Where did you get that c-u-u-ute shirt, dude? Your mommy buy it for you?"

And Tyler looked very surprised and said, "Why, no, G.G. I borrowed it from you. Don't you remember?"

But one thing G.G. didn't do anymore was imitate Libby by scurrying to his seat and hiding behind a book. He stopped doing that all of a sudden after Libby came in the door one day and he started doing his imitation and something—perhaps it was watching Tyler and Dawn—gave her the courage to imitate him back. When everyone had finished watching G.G. and turned to look to see how Libby was taking it, she did the same thing only even more exaggeratedly. Everyone laughed—only this time it was *with* instead of *at* Libby, and that must have spoiled it for G.G., because from then on he didn't do it anymore.

It was one Wednesday morning in mid-April when Libby ran into G.G. in the hall on her way to math class. When he saw her, he headed in her direction, and she braced herself for some new kind of torture, but for once he seemed to have something else on his mind.

"Hey, McBrain," he said. "You hear the good news? The O lady is missing."

"What do you mean?" Libby said, trying to edge past him.

"I mean there probably isn't going to be any ol' workee-shoppee this afternoon, because Madame O is gone—absent —out to lunch. I have her for English first period and we had a substitute this morning."

"Well, there'll still be a workshop, won't there?" Libby said. "The substitute will just take Mizzo's place."

G.G. shrugged and said, "Yeah, maybe," and walked off.

Libby didn't like the idea of having someone else running the FFW workshop, but since it wouldn't be her turn to read anyway, she didn't mind all that much. And having the substitute would be better than just canceling it. At noon she talked to Tierney and Alex, and they both agreed that the substitute would probably take charge of the workshop too. "That's part of her job," Tierney said.

"Yes," Alex said. "Mizzo wouldn't let her substitute cut the workshop. I think it's probably her favorite class."

"Yeah," Tierney said, "She wouldn't let anything interfere with her 'incredible' FFW."

But it seemed that Alex and Tierney were both wrong, because when the bell rang for the beginning of seventh period, there was no substitute in the reading lab, and five minutes later she still hadn't arrived.

At first everyone just waited and talked. Tierney was telling Alex that she was going to read today and if he even so much as *thought* of the word *parody,* she was going to borrow one of G.G.'s laser guns and reduce him to very fine ash. And Wendy was telling Libby about the new story she

146

had just started that took place in the 1920s. After a while G.G. got up and put his binder back into his backpack.

"I don't know about you dudes," he said. "But I'm outta here."

He was almost to the door when Tierney said, "Hey G. Man. Where do you think you're going? You might as well stay here. You can't leave the school grounds until three-twenty anyway."

Holding the door open with one hand, G.G. turned around with a lip-twisting sneer on his pudgy, freckled face —and just at that minute another face appeared in the doorway right above his. It was Mr. Shoemaker, the principal.

"Sure I can," G.G. said. "I do it all the time. Over the fence behind the gym. You just climb up the drainpipe at the corner of the building until you're as high as . . ." His voice faltered as he began to realize that the other FFW members were staring past him—instead of at him. "As high as . . ." he said again in a tight voice and whirled around to find himself face-to-face with the principal.

"I see," Mr. Shoemaker said, taking hold of G.G.'s shoulder and steering him back into the room. "I'm glad to hear that that's how it's done. I guess we're going to have to do something about that drainpipe. And now, if you'll just take a seat, Mr. Greene, I've a sad duty to perform.

"Ms. Ostrowski," Mr. Shoemaker told them in a solemn voice, "was involved in an automobile accident on her way home from school last night. Quite a bad one, I'm afraid." Libby felt a stillness inside, as if for just an instant everything stopped working, and then started up again in gasps and thuds as Mr. Shoemaker went on talking.

"Oh, she's going to be all right eventually," he said,

147

"but she has several badly broken bones, and her doctor tells us she'll be in the hospital for quite a while."

They sat there, all of them, in stunned silence, staring first at Mr. Shoemaker and then at each other. Libby kept thinking of Mizzo sitting there in her usual place in the circle, looking the way she always did, smiling her enthusiastic smile with her long cat eyes tipping up at the corners. And now there was a new picture in her mind—Mizzo in a hospital bed with huge casts on her arms and legs and . . . "What bones?" she asked. "What did Mizzo, I mean Ms. Ostrowski, break?"

But Mr. Shoemaker had started talking about something else and didn't hear her question. ". . . and since the sponsorship of this club was an added responsibility that Ms. Ostrowski volunteered to take on and not actually part of her job responsibilities, we can't insist that Mrs. Granger fill in. So I'm afraid, for the time being, you'll all have to return to your previous Creative Choice assignments."

No one spoke for several seconds, and then Alex raised his hand. "Mr. Shoemaker," he said. "Couldn't we just go ahead without a sponsor? I mean, we all know the routine now, and we could just—"

"No, I'm afraid not," the principal said. "We can't allow students to use school facilities without an adult being present. It's against the rules."

Wendy stood up. "But, sir," she said, her smile polished and positive, "we've just started this collaboration. I mean, this story that we're all contributing to, and it's very important to all of us. Couldn't we go on meeting just a few more times until we finish the story?"

For a moment Libby felt reassured. It just didn't seem

possible that anyone could refuse such a confident request. But as it turned out, Mr. Shoemaker could and did, and a few minutes later they were all out in the hall watching the principal lock the door to the reading lab. Then he told them again how sorry he was to have to dissolve the writers' workshop and that they should all go along now to their previous clubs or lessons and tell the teachers why they were there. "They've all heard about Ms. Ostrowski's unfortunate accident," he said, "so they'll understand." He took a list out of his pocket and after studying it for a moment, he said, "Let's see. Gary and Alex were in the Journalism Club, Libby was in Great Books, Tierney was in the Historical Society, and Wendy met with the Student Government Club. So, if you'll all just report back, I'm sure you'll be given a sympathetic welcome." Then he gave all of them what was obviously meant to be a sympathetic smile, put the reading-lab key back in his pocket, and hurried off down the hall.

They all stood there for a minute longer, staring at the locked door, the way Gill's cats always stared at the kitchen door at dinnertime. G.G. was the first one to speak. "Hey," he said. "I been wanting out of this little"—he made his voice high and fluty and put on what he obviously meant to be a haughty expression— "lit-ter-aree so-ci-itee for a long time. So—no problem. Right?"

"Oh, shut up, G.G.," Alex said. They all stared at Alex in surprise. It wasn't the kind of thing Alex usually said. And certainly not the kind of thing he usually said to G.G.

"Hey. Way to go, Lockwood," Tierney said, grinning, and after a minute Alex stopped frowning and grinned too.

"Sorry," he said to G.G. "But I'm just so—mad. What gives them the right to say we can't go on meeting? I mean, isn't it in the Constitution or something? The right to free assembly, or something like that."

"Yes, you're right," Wendy said. "I learned about it in civics. Americans are supposed to have the right to have meetings whenever and wherever they want to."

Libby sighed. "I guess it's the wherever that's the problem. We can't meet on the school grounds without an adult to—"

"Hey!" Wendy almost shouted. "That's right. We just can't meet *here.* But we could go on having our workshop *somewhere else.*" She was staring at Libby with what, if you were Alex Lockwood, you would probably call "wild surmise"—a thought that might have made Libby laugh, if she hadn't begun to have a sneaking suspicion that she knew exactly what Wendy was surmising. And she wasn't the only one. Alex and Tierney were both staring at Libby, too, with excited, hopeful eyes.

"I don't know," she began slowly. "I'll have to ask. I'll have to ask the family and—"

"Hey, no problem," Tierney said, "and you know it. Or you ought to anyway. You've got that whole McCall House gang wrapped around your itty-bitty finger. If *you* want us to meet at the McCall House, you got it. Right?"

Libby couldn't help smiling. "Well, I guess so," she said.

"Hoo-ray! She guesses so," Alex said. "Libby McCall, who, by the way, ladies and gentlemen, is a world-class guesser, guesses that we can meet at her fantastic, awesome, humongous house. All in favor say aye."

150

"Aye!" they all—except maybe for G.G.—said, and then all of them—even G.G.—crowded around Libby asking her questions about when they could have the first workshop meeting at the McCall House.

16

So it was decided. The next meeting of the workshop would take place at the McCall House, but that still left the time to be decided upon. It seemed that Saturdays and Sundays were out because so many people went away or had other important plans for their weekends. Thursday afternoons wouldn't do because Wendy had afterschool cheerleader practice. Tierney's orthodontist was on Tuesdays. And Alex had a regular clinic appointment on Monday afternoons. So they were back to Wednesdays, but now it would have to be after school instead of during seventh period. But when Libby said, "All right. Next Wednesday. At my house," Alex grinned and said, "How about this Wednesday, in about"—he looked at his wristwatch—"in about forty minutes. That gives everybody just about enough time to check it out with their parents. Okay?"

So instead of going immediately to their previous Creative Choice classes, as Mr. Shoemaker had suggested, they went down together to the pay phone and started calling home. Everyone except G.G., who went with them but then just stood around watching and listening. When Libby asked him if he wasn't going to call, he said, "No. Like I told you, I've been wanting to get out of this dweep convention for a long time. And I got better things to do after school." But for some reason he went on standing around listening while everyone talked to their parents.

They let Libby call first, and Gillian answered and said of course the workshop could meet there and she thought it was a wonderful idea. And the rest of them got permission without much difficulty, except that Wendy had to tell her mother exactly who was going to be there and exactly how and when she'd be getting home.

"Yes," she said. "Tierney and Libby will be there too. Yes, I have enough money for the bus." She looked at Libby and sighed and rolled her eyes in a way that said something about nosy parents, but she went on answering all her mother's questions, and before she hung up, she said, "Bye, Mom. Thanks. See you in a couple of hours."

Tierney's conversation was much shorter, and she didn't ask for permission as much as announce what she was going to do. The last thing she said was, "On the bus. Yeah. Okay. Okay!" And then she hung up and turned the phone over to Alex.

Alex's parents apparently weren't at home, but he had an interesting conversation with their answering machine. "Hello there, Machine, old buddy," he said. "Nice to talk to you again. Would you be so kind as to tell my honorable parents that the writers' workshop will have to be held after —that's *after* as in 'following' or 'subsequent to'—the school day, so I'll be late getting home. Oh, and Machine. The workshop is being held today at the McCall mansion."

He stopped for a minute and pretended to be listening before he said, "I knew you'd be impressed. But, no, I'm afraid you can't come along. It's a very exclusive group. Humans only. No machines allowed."

It was just a little later, while they were all checking to be sure they had enough money to take the bus, that G.G. disappeared. Libby didn't notice him leaving, but one minute he was standing there watching and the next moment he wasn't. But when she said, "What happened to G.G.," the others just glanced around, shrugged, and went back to counting their money. Nobody said anything except for Tierney, who said, "Good riddance—twenty-three, twenty-four . . . Hey, I'm a penny short. Anybody got a spare penny?"

They split up then and went off to their old Creative Choice assignments, but right after school let out, they met again on the front steps and walked to the bus stop together.

The bus was crowded that day and they weren't able to sit close enough to do much talking, but at one point Tierney, who was sitting several rows ahead of Libby, climbed over the large man who was sitting next to her and came down the aisle. She stopped to whisper to Wendy, who immediately turned around and began nodding her head frantically. Then Tierney came on down to Libby's seat and, putting her hands around her mouth, whispered, "The Treehouse. We're going to have the meeting in the Treehouse, aren't we?"

Libby's immediate reaction was to shake her head. It wasn't anything rational or planned, as much as it was an almost frightened feeling. A quick, deep negative feeling about having something so public in such a private place.

But, on second thought, when she realized that there would only be three people besides herself, and two of them had already been in the Treehouse, she began to change her mind. So eventually the head shake turned into an uncertain, tentative nod.

Immediately Wendy bounced up and down, doing her best wide-screen smile, and Tierney yelled, "All right!" so loudly that several people nearly jumped out of their seats. Alex, who couldn't have known what they'd been talking about, turned around and echoed Tierney's "all right." All of which, for some reason, inspired a bunch of elementary school kids in the back of the bus to start yelling "all right!" too. So then Tierney stomped back up the aisle, making okay signs over her head and chanting, "All right, all right," until she got to her row and climbed back over the large man into her seat.

The people in Libby's row were staring at her, making her feel embarrassed but at the same time rather pleased with herself. Pleased that they were probably wondering about all the "all rights" and what she had said or done to set them off.

She still didn't feel entirely at ease about having the meeting in the Treehouse, however, but there was no chance to discuss it any further. The only other conversations on the bus were a few remarks that were passed around from one person to another about how much more peaceful the workshop was going to be minus "you know who."

But then, just as they arrived at the McCall House, "you know who" suddenly showed up again—like an evil genie who kept escaping just when you thought he was cooped up forever in his bottle. They were just going in the front gate when they became aware of someone shouting, and there he was racing toward them on his bicycle, yelling, "Hey! Wait up! Wait for me!"

As they waited, with Tierney groaning and Wendy saying something to Alex about being afraid it was too good to be true, Libby discovered that she was experiencing a strange mixture of feelings. There was the angry exasperation she would have expected over G.G.'s managing to upset things as usual. And there was also the anxiety about having him see the house and meet her family, all of which would just give him that much more to sneer about. But there was something else. Another reaction that felt more like relief. Relief that she'd get another chance to find out something—to satisfy a strange, urgent kind of curiosity that had been tickling somewhere inside her head ever since the day that G.G. read the unfinished story called "Eric."

The others came back out onto the sidewalk, groaning and shaking their heads, and a minute later Gary Greene skidded his bicycle to a stop almost on top of them. His freckled face was red and sweaty, and he was grinning triumphantly.

"Well, well," Tierney said. "To what do we owe this honor, G. Man? Something happen to all those better things you had to do?"

"Yeah, that's it," G.G. said, in between panting breaths. "When I got home, I found out I didn't have some other things to do after all. So I just decided to see if I could beat the old bus over here. I almost made it too. Get out of the way, Lockwood. I want to put my bike inside the fence so it won't get stolen." Shoving his bike toward the gate, he bumped it into Alex, making him stumble back against the fence.

"Watch it," Alex said, grabbing the fence to keep from falling down.

"Yeah! Watch it!" Tierney grabbed the back of G.G.'s bicycle and jerked it so hard he lost his grip and it shot backward and fell to the ground with a clatter. He whirled around, glaring, his shoulders hunched and his fists clenched. Tierney glared back, and they were moving toward each other when Libby stepped in between them.

"Look," she yelled at G.G., knowing that what she was doing was ridiculous and dangerous, but somehow not caring. "Just stop it. This is my house, and if you don't stop it this minute, I'll—I'll throw you out."

For a minute he glared down—way down—at her, and then slowly he began to grin. Somebody—it sounded like Alex—made a smothered-laughter noise, and Tierney said, "Go for it, Mighty Mouse. Punch him out."

G.G.'s grin widened, and suddenly Libby giggled. Then she held up her clenched fists and bounced around like a prizefighter, and then they were all laughing—even G.G. In fact G.G. laughed hardest of all, in a strange, out-of-control way that made you wonder if he was going to be able to stop. He was still making occasional snorting noises a few minutes later as they all filed through the double doors into the huge entry hall of the McCall House.

Nobody seemed to be home. Wendy wanted to tour the house again, and of course G.G. hadn't seen it, so they went through the library and study and Great Hall once more. This time Wendy and Tierney did most of the talking, pointing out things like the chandeliers and balconies. G.G.

157

hardly said anything. His grin had slipped back into a sneer, and the only thing he said was something about the house looking haunted and to ask Libby if she was going to introduce them to the ghosts. Alex didn't say much either, at least not until Gillian and Cordelia finally showed up.

Alex, as Libby had noticed before, was always in top form with adults. When Cordelia came in through the kitchen—she'd been downtown buying some cookies—and Gillian, wearing her practice leotards, came down the back stairs from her studio, where she'd been doing her ballet exercises, Alex immediately became a kind of master of ceremonies. The first thing he did was introduce G.G.

"And this is our fellow workshop member, Gary Greene," he told Gillian and Cordelia. "Otherwise known as G.G. G.G. is a very talented writer. Besides which he is a perfect . . ." He stopped and scratched his head. "I'm having trouble thinking of just the right word," he said, but his smile said that he knew exactly what he'd like to say. "A perfect . . ." Grinning and rolling his eyes wildly, he turned to Tierney. "A perfect . . . ?" he said again, making it into a question.

"Got it!" Tierney said. "G.G. is a perfect—no—no—I guess not. Not when there are ladies present."

Everyone laughed, and Cordelia said, "Gentleman. I'm sure the word is *gentleman,*" which of course sent them all into hysterics.

The cats came in then and started showing off, with Goliath weaving himself around people's ankles and Isadora chasing Ariel up the draperies. By the time Cordelia brought out the cookies and lemonade, G.G. had started saying that he was going to have to leave soon, so they ate and drank quickly and headed for the Treehouse.

As they left the kitchen, Libby was still feeling a vague resistance to the thought of outsiders, particularly a certain outsider, in her Treehouse, but she soon had other things to think about. And by the time the whole group had finally settled down to work in the main room of the Treehouse, it was beginning to seem almost normal to have them there.

We didn't get any actual critiquing done at all, Libby wrote in her journal that night. *At first the Treehouse took up a lot of time. Everyone except Alex, who had trouble even getting to the first floor, had to explore the other levels. Then I stupidly mentioned that I could go back and forth to the Treehouse from my balcony, and G.G. insisted on trying to do it. The good news is—he couldn't. I noticed right away that the trouble was his weight. He weighs a lot more than I do, and when he went up the last limb, it bent way down, so there was no way he could reach the balcony rail. I didn't point out what the problem was, however. Just let him go on thinking that I'm a much better climber.*

Then, just as we were almost ready to start, Goliath and Ariel came in the window and interrupted things, but after that we at least got a little business taken care of.

The first thing we did was choose a chairperson. It was Wendy's idea. She said we'd have to have someone to call on people and decide who reads next, and do the other things Mizzo used to do. I think Wendy thought she'd be elected. But Alex nominated me, and guess what?—I won. I think Wendy was surprised. I know I was.

159

Then I appointed Wendy secretary, and everyone helped dictate a get-well note for Mizzo. Then we discussed going to the hospital together to see her, and I appointed Tierney chairman in charge of finding out about visiting the hospital and sending the get-well note and maybe some flowers too. By then it was already getting late, and G.G. kept asking what time it was and saying he had to go, so all we did was make some plans about the next "Island Adventure" episode, and then they all went home.

After she'd finished describing the meeting, Libby still felt like writing. She'd written about the people in the work-shop before, in short bits and pieces, but now she suddenly decided to do one of Mizzo's character sketches on each one of them. She got four copies of the character-sketch form out of her book bag and added them to the green notebook. After several minutes of thought she wrote *Gary Greene* at the top of the first one.

She didn't know why she decided to do G.G. first, since he was obviously her least favorite—the only one, actually, whom she still hated. But it had something to do with the way she'd felt when he showed up on his bicycle. As if there were something strange and unexplained about him. Some-thing that gave her the same eager, expectant curiosity that made her look into windows and over fences.

But when she started going through the character-sketch form, she found there were a great many things about him that she still didn't know. She filled out the ques-tions about physical characteristics, such as eye and hair color *(brown and blondish brown)* and size and body type *(large and muscular),* but she had almost no answers for the family questions. Alex had told her that G.G.'s father had once been a professional football player and that his parents were divorced, but other than that she knew nothing at all about his home life.

When she came to the checklist about mental and emotional characteristics, she put checks after *Intelligent* and *Talented* and double checks after *Aggressive, Cruel,* and *Violent.* In the blank space labeled "Other," she quickly wrote *frightened*—followed by several question marks.

17

Tierney did a lot of complaining about how much work it had been to make the arrangements for the hospital visit. Listening to all her fussing and fuming, a person who didn't know her very well might have thought she really hated having to do it. In fact it took Libby herself, who had learned a lot about Tierney Laurent, a little while to catch on. To realize that she was really enjoying it—checking with the other members of the group, doing all the planning and phoning, and making important decisions. Particularly making the decisions. She was really into that part of it. But all week long she went on telling everyone how the whole thing had stressed her out.

"Like picking out this stupid get-well card," she told Libby. "I had to go to three or four different places because most of the cards were so dorky, I mean, like, completely brain dead or else total barf. And then in Langley's Stationery it took me so long to decide, this prissy little dude of a clerk started harshing on me, like he thought I was trying to steal one of his dorky cards. But then I found this one.

What do you think? The picture is sort of Mizzo, don't you think?"

The picture was okay, a glamorous-looking woman sitting up in bed, but inside it only said, "Hope you'll soon be feeling as great as you look," so Libby sat down cross-legged on the lawn—they were hanging out in their favorite lunch-hour spot in the north patio at the time—and wrote a limerick. It went:

> *We're sending this card to Mizzo,*
> *Cause we thought she just might like to know,*
> *The* INCREDIBLE FIVE.
> Have plans to survive,
> Though her absence has been a great blow.

When they read it, Wendy said it was really rad, and Tierney said she thought that Libby had a great future as a verse writer for Hallmark. But then she said, "No, it's great. A real killer. I don't know how you do that, just off the top that way. Now if we can get Miss Student Government here to copy it into the card with her natural-born class-secretary handwriting, we'll be all set to fly."

So Wendy copied the limerick into the card and while she was doing it, Tierney went on about how buying the card was only the beginning of her troubles. There had been ordering the flowers and collecting the money to buy them and then arranging the trip to the hospital. Especially arranging the trip to the hospital.

Mizzo, it seemed, belonged to a health plan whose hospital was in the city, so she'd been transferred there from the one she'd been taken to in Morrison. And getting the whole FFW to San Francisco was going to be a real bummer.

"My mom offered to drive us in," Tierney said, "if everyone can go on Saturday. The only trouble is our car only holds five people, and with her driving that adds up to six."

Wendy giggled. "Couldn't we tie G.G. on the roof?" she said.

"Yeah," Tierney said. "As in hog-tie. Great idea."

"Or in the trunk?" Libby said. "I think the trunk would be a perfect place for him."

But the way it turned out, finding a spot for G.G. wasn't necessary. G.G. couldn't, or perhaps didn't want to, go. So they were down to four people—five counting Mrs. Laurent—and then Alex had to back out too. His parents were going to Carmel that weekend, and Alex had to go with them. So, on Saturday morning only the three female members of the FFW met at the Laurents' house to make the trip to San Francisco.

Except for a couple of casts and a bandage on her head, Mizzo seemed just the same as always, cheerful and enthusiastic. She seemed to be a favorite of the nurses, and several of them came in to be introduced. She told all of them that her visitors—Libby, Wendy, and Tierney—were all incredibly talented writers and that the nurses should write down their names and remember them because they'd probably all be published and famous before very long.

They talked for almost an hour, and Mizzo wanted to know how they all were and what they were working on and how the "Island Adventure" was going. And when Tierney and Wendy told her about meeting in Libby's Treehouse, she got really excited and said she hoped they could meet there at least once more after she was back in the group.

When Libby asked her how her own novel was going, she said it hadn't been going anywhere until a couple of days ago when her father brought her the manuscript and a new lap-sized computer. She had already started putting the novel on disk, she said, and even though she could only use one hand, she was making rapid progress. And she entirely agreed with Alex that word processors were the only way to go.

Just before they left, she asked about G.G., so they told her about how he had said he was going to quit when Mr. Shoemaker threw them out of the reading lab and then showed up unexpectedly at the McCall House.

She nodded slowly then, with a worried look on her face, and said, "Don't let him quit, girls. He needs the workshop. I think G.G. really needs—all of us."

None of them, not even Tierney, said anything nonconstructive about G.G. to Mizzo, but later when they were on their way back down to the parking lot to meet Mrs. Laurent, Tierney snorted and said, "He needs us? That's a laugh. I don't know what G.G. needs us for, unless he's lost his punching bag, or something. And all I can say is that, for a really sharp person, Mizzo can certainly go dim on you at times."

That night in her Wednesday journal Libby wrote: *An outrageous day. I mean, really rad.* That was what Wendy had said about the trip, that it was "like, outrageous, a really rad day." *We went to the hospital and then we had lunch at Fisherman's Wharf and went through the Exploratorium before we started home. Wendy really seemed to have a great time. And Tierney did too, I think. Tierney was different anyway. She actually talked to her mother a little. And something else about Tierney, her hair isn't pink anymore. Actually it's more like purple now, but she says the purple is just an in-between stage so everyone won't go into culture shock when she goes back to plain old brown.*

Wendy seemed different too. Well, maybe not. Maybe it was more I see different things about her now. Tierney said she did too. That was after we got back to Morrison and Mrs. Laurent dropped Wendy off at her house. After Wendy got out of the car, I made some comment about Wendy, and Tierney said that she used to think that Wendy Davis was just a bubble-headed phony and that all that nicey-nice stuff was just an act. Then what Tierney actually said was, word-for-word—"I was sure she was just faking it, because most 'in-groupers' don't go around smiling at nerds and dweeps, and really mean it—you know, nerds like me and dweeps like you."

She was laughing when she said that last part, but I didn't think it was all that funny. Then she shrugged and said, "But now I think maybe she isn't such a phony after all."

I told Tierney that I thought so too. That is, I never did really think Wendy was a phony, or bubble-headed either. It seemed to me that it was more a kind of ignorance—about different kinds of ideas and other kinds of people, too. Like in her stories when she wrote very well—but only about boring subjects. It was like she always had it so easy—being born extraordinarily talented and beautiful in a rather ordinary family, she just never realized there were people with real

166

problems. And when you come right down to it, people with-
out any real problems are pretty uninteresting to write about.

On Monday Alex came to the McCall House again
to visit Gillian and Cordelia. At least that's what he said.
And he certainly spent most of the time talking to them.
But just before he went home, he did ask Libby if he could
go look at the Treehouse again.

"Why?" Libby asked.

"Because it is such an absolutely unreal place," he said.
"I want to see it again when all those other people aren't
around. You know, muscle-bound types like Tierney and
G.G. I want to see if I can climb up to the other rooms."

So they went out to the Treehouse, and at first Alex just
sat in the main room looking around the way he'd done in
the big house. Then, after he'd raved for a while about what
an unbelievable place it was, he climbed up to the other
rooms. It wasn't easy for him, and sometimes he had to sit
down on a stair and scoot up backward, but he didn't want
any help and he finally made it to the highest room and
back.

When he came down to the main room again, he asked
Libby why she hadn't told him about the Treehouse when
he was there the first time.

"Because it was a secret," she told him. "I didn't intend
to show it to anybody, ever. But then I kind of let Tierney
and Wendy find out about it and I had to show it to them. I
didn't want to, but I had to."

"Yeah, I can see it all now," Alex said. "Saying no to
those two wouldn't have been easy. They're both pretty

167

used to getting their own way, I think. Like, Tierney just plain throws her weight around, and Wendy does it with a sugar coating, but the results are pretty much the same."

Libby sighed, "I know. And then, when G.G. turned up, I *really* didn't want to have the meeting up here, but it was too late by then."

Alex nodded. "Yeah. I hear you," he said. "Gary Greene is not the kind of guy—" He stopped there and it was quite a while before he went on. "—You know what? I'm not so sure anymore just what kind of guy old G.G. is. I mean, just when he's been doing his public-enemy-number-one bit, it's like he loses his grip and suddenly there's this almost-human person. I mean, this person looking at you like, 'Help, let me out of here.' "

Libby opened her mouth in amazement, closed it, and finally just nodded—because Alex had said almost exactly what she'd been thinking without ever quite putting it into words. But later she told Alex that she really agreed with him. That she sometimes felt there was something hidden and mysterious about G.G. But by then Alex seemed to have changed his mind. "Sure," he said. "Old G.G. is pretty mysterious, all right. Like, the mystery is, how did anyone get to be so mean in just thirteen years?"

On the next Wednesday afternoon everyone except G.G. rode the Westwind bus to the McCall House again, but this time G.G. told them ahead of time that he would be coming later.

"I have something I have to do first," he'd told Libby

and Wendy, who were waiting for the others in front of the school—in the pouring rain. Libby was sharing Wendy's umbrella, and G.G., in a large yellow slicker, was just getting ready to get on his bicycle. At first he was definitely in one of his better moods.

"It won't take long," he said. "Then I'll catch the next bus or else ride my bike again. Just leave the gate unlocked and I'll be there as soon as I can. Okay?"

Libby said okay even though Wendy punched her and rolled her eyes in a "do we have to?" expression. But then something made G.G. angry—maybe he caught Wendy's look—and his usual dangerous grin returned.

"Or not," he said. "You can lock me out if you want to. Climbing that broken-down fence wouldn't be any problem. And now that I know where it is, I can visit your super-secret Treehouse anytime I want to. Maybe make a little late-night visit sometime. Bring a few tools and do a little remodeling, maybe."

Trying to ignore the lump that thudded into the pit of her stomach, Libby answered as calmly as she could. "We won't lock you out. Just come on in the gate and around to the Treehouse."

He stared at her for a moment, his grin gradually changing back from evil to almost human, before he jumped on his bicycle and tore off through the rain, splashing water all over several pedestrians and almost running over a passing dachshund. Libby and Wendy stared at each other, shaking their heads.

Alex and Tierney appeared a minute later, and they all started off together. It was a spring-storm day, not terribly cold but extremely windy, and they arrived at the McCall House wet and windblown and chilly. Once inside the fence, Libby immediately headed toward the Treehouse path, but the others hung back, staring up from under their umbrellas at the rainswept stone walls. She knew what they were thinking. It was McCall House weather, the kind of wild, gray day that turned the house into the setting for some ancient tale of mystery, a dark castle looming against a cloudy sky.

"Come on. Let's go," she was urging them, when Gillian appeared in the doorway. Elliott, it seemed, had come home early and was in the kitchen baking gingerbread. Libby tried to say they didn't have time, but no one listened, and a few minutes later the four of them were sitting around the kitchen table drinking hot chocolate and eating huge slabs of fresh gingerbread, while Elliott asked questions about the FFW and everyone's work-in-progress.

It was the first time that any of them had met Elliott, and Libby hadn't really been sorry they'd missed him. Even though he was such a great person, she'd been sure that they'd think he was just one more weird difference, another thing that didn't fit into the usual pattern and therefore one more thing to poke fun at. But now, watching them telling Elliott—through mouthfuls of gingerbread—about the stories they were working on, she began to relax. She could tell they liked him.

And watching Elliott talking—to Tierney now—his gray eyes under the exclamation-mark eyebrows, level and intent, she wondered what she'd been worried about.

Elliott was in the pantry putting away the remaining

gingerbread, and Gillian had gone back up to her studio, when the phone rang, and went on ringing.

Libby hated to let phones ring unanswered. Christopher said her mad dashes to the telephone were because she was afraid of missing a call from her fairy godmother, but of course that wasn't really the reason. Perhaps it was a matter of not wanting to miss something, however—not wanting to miss knowing who was calling and why and what kind of news they might have. Which, of course, was all just a part of her writer's curiosity. But this time, sitting there at the kitchen table with the rest of the FFW, she forced herself to wait—for someone else to answer it.

Of course Christopher often ignored telephones, and in her studio with the music playing, Gillian might not hear it. But it wasn't until Elliott stuck his head out of the pantry and asked Libby to get the phone that she remembered that Cordelia was away, visiting in San Francisco. As she leaped to her feet and dashed out of the room, Libby heard people laughing and Tierney yelling, "Go for it, Mighty Mouse," but she kept going and picked up the phone on what must have been the ninth or tenth ring.

At first no one answered her breathless "Hello, McCall residence," but then a whispering voice said something she couldn't quite catch.

"What?" she said. "Could you speak louder? I can't hear you."

There was a pause, and then the voice came again, still whispering, but this time loud enough for her to hear. "It's me. G.G. I just wanted to tell you I won't be there. I can't get away. I mean, I—"

Then suddenly there was the sound of yelling—a deep

171

voice shouting something about the telephone, and someone, perhaps G.G., shouting, "No. Don't. I wasn't calling
them. I wasn't—no. Don't. Please!"

There were other sounds then, thuds and crashes and a
deafening clatter as if the phone had crashed to the floor.
And then the line went dead.

18

"Hello! Hello! G.G. What happened, G.G.?" Libby almost shouted, but there was no answer. At last she slowly put the phone back in its cradle—and stood staring at it, willing G.G. to call back and explain everything. But the phone remained silent and after a while she gave up on waiting for it to ring and began to search for possible explanations of what she had heard. But the search was hampered by a kind of resistance that made her mind keep skidding away from some of the possibilities.

At last she shook her head hard and said, "No. It was probably just that his dad was yelling about something and he dropped the phone. That's all it was." Nodding briskly—as if she were sure she had arrived at the right answer—she started back toward the kitchen. But partway through the Great Hall she began to hear an echo, an echo of shouting, and of G.G.'s pleading voice, and by the time she reached the kitchen, the words "No. Don't. Please" were throbbing through her mind like electrical pulses.

Alex and Tierney and Wendy were still sitting at the

table, but as Libby entered the room they turned to look at her and immediately stopped talking and laughing. "What is it?" Tierney said. "What's the matter?"

"I'm not sure," Libby said in a quavering voice. "It was G.G. I think something's happened to G.G. Where's Elliott? I think I'd better tell Elliott."

"He left," Alex said. "Just a minute ago. He told us to tell you he'd forgotten something he had to do at the store. He'd said he'd be back in an hour or so."

"Oh, no!" Libby said, and without waiting to explain, she dashed out of the room, through the service porch, and out into the drive—just in time to see Elliott's Toyota disappearing down Westwind.

Back again in the kitchen, she suddenly felt angry— angry at Elliott for running off without telling her and at all of them, sitting there at the table as if it wasn't their problem and they didn't intend to do anything about it.

So she told them exactly what she'd heard, how G.G. had whispered that he couldn't come and then how he had screamed, "No. Don't. Please," before the noises started and the phone went dead. "We've got to go," she said then. "We have to go help him."

She started out to the hallway and they followed, but when she started putting on her raincoat, they all just stood there staring at her as if they couldn't decide what to do.

"Aren't you going to tell your grandmother?" Wendy asked.

Libby nodded and started for the stairs, but then she came back. "I don't think I will. There's no other car, so she couldn't take us, and if she decides to go with us, it will take forever. It would take her ages to get ready. And she won't miss us. If she comes back downstairs, she'll just think we're in the Treehouse."

"Okay," Alex said, "but don't you think we ought to call someone first?" Alex said finally, "Like maybe the police."

Tierney shook her head. "I don't think we should call the police. I mean, what if nothing really bad was happening? Nothing bad enough to call the police about, anyway. I'll bet if we call the police, we'll just get G.G. in more trouble, and ourselves too."

It was Wendy who finally asked if anyone knew where G.G. lived, and when Alex said he did, she nodded and picked up her coat. "Well, come on, then," she said. "Let's get going." That settled it. No one argued anymore, as if having someone as proper and respectable as Wendy suggest it made it a safe and reasonable thing to do. Without any more discussion they all got into their coats and slickers and started out the door.

The rain had stopped for the time being, but the sky was still dark, and the wind was howling through Morrison, tossing treetops and sailing bits of debris on invisible currents. Pushing against the wind on their way to the bus stop, no one even tried to talk, and in the packed rush-hour bus, there was no opportunity. And when, squeezed in between two very tall adults, Libby tried to discuss it with herself, her interior dialogue got nowhere. Or at least not to any useful decisions or conclusions. Questions about what they might find when they got to G.G.'s and what they might do about it got only the same useless answer: "We just have to see if he's all right." The same words were still

175

spinning pointlessly through her head when she heard Alex calling to her, "Next stop. Get off at the next stop."

It was an old Morrison neighborhood, with large, well-built houses, many of them in an imitation Spanish-hacienda style. The one Alex led them to had thickly stuccoed walls, a red tiled roof, and wrought-iron bars over the windows. The yard had once been carefully landscaped with clusters of cactus plants, stone benches beside graveled paths, and in the center of a large circle of lawn, an enormous terra cotta fountain. But the lawn was ragged and weed-grown, and the house looked weather-stained and neglected, with the windows draped or shuttered against the light.

They stood close together at the beginning of the curving path that led to the front door, as if waiting for a signal, or for someone to make the first move.

"Neat house," Tierney said finally. "Kind of run-down, though. You been here before, Alex?"

Alex nodded. "Yes, once or twice. A long time ago. When the Greenes first came to town. Gary—G.G., that is —and I were both at Lincoln Primary then, and for a little while we were kind of halfway friends, believe it or not. That was in the second grade. His dad is Tony Greene. Used to be a famous football player. My dad remembers seeing him play. But that was a long time ago. When he quit playing, he came back here to take over the family business, or something."

Libby had already heard about Alex and G.G. being friends in the second grade, but apparently the others hadn't. They stared at Alex, nodding eagerly, as if encouraging him to go on. As if standing there in a windblown clump, listening to Alex talk, was just exactly what they'd come all the way across town to do. But Alex didn't have anything more to say, so they just went on standing there, looking at each other and then at the silent, dark-windowed house.

The wind was at their backs now, and they all seemed to be leaning against it, as if to keep it from shoving them forward down the curving path. When they finally began to move, it was all at once, as if caught and carried forward by a sudden, stronger gust.

They were already moving when Tierney said, "Forward march, troops. The FFW riot squad to the rescue." Her voice sounded normal, amused, and scornful, but the sarcastic grin that usually went with it was missing, and her face looked tense and stiff. Alex looked grim, too, pale and solemn and even more nervous than usual.

Only Wendy seemed herself, not smiling but calm and confident, and for just a moment Libby felt comforted— until she realized why Wendy didn't seem to be as frightened as the rest of them. It was just, as Libby had decided before, that Wendy was too used to a world where everything had always been safe and easy. But this wasn't Wendy's world, and this time there might not be anything to be calm and confident about. That thought was anything but comforting, and for just a second Libby wanted to grab Wendy's arm and pull her back. "Look out," she wanted to say. "Look out, Wendy." But she didn't say or do anything —so it was Wendy who marched right across the porch and rang the doorbell.

"Well, let's get this over with," she said in a businesslike

177

tone of voice as she pressed firmly on the button and then moved quickly back into line with the others.

Alex laughed nervously and said, "Trick or treat," and the others laughed, too, weakly, and then went silent, listening and waiting. Nothing happened.

"Maybe it isn't working," Wendy said.

"No, it's working, all right. I heard it—I think," Tierney said. "Here. I'll do it."

So Tierney tried the bell, and they all came closer to listen, and sure enough, you could hear it chiming faintly somewhere deep inside the house. But nothing happened and no one came to the door.

"Well, I guess no one's home," Wendy said. "I guess we might as well go." The others nodded, looking relieved, and began to move away toward the steps and the path beyond. Libby was moving away, too, thinking, Yes, we might as well go, when she heard it echoing again inside her head— the words she had heard on the telephone. Turning back, she grabbed the heavy bronze door latch with both hands and pushed hard, and the door swung open.

The hallway was wide, with a domed ceiling and a floor of handmade Mexican tiles. In the dim light it was just possible to make out a narrow table against one wall and a hand-carved antique bench against another. To the left was a closed double door, but to the right an open archway let in a pale column of light. As Libby stepped forward into the hall, she heard footsteps behind her and felt someone brush against her arm. The others were coming too.

The double doors led to a living room, full of heavy Spanish-style furniture. There was a round-topped fireplace in one corner, and two large wagon-wheel chandeliers hung from the beamed ceiling. There was a heavy, musty smell of tobacco, and the room was littered with papers, magazines, glasses, and overflowing ashtrays. Shutters were closed over most of the windows, and nothing stirred in the dim light.

Retreating backward into the hall, Libby bumped into Wendy, who grabbed her by the back of her coat and pulled her toward the front door. "Come on," she whispered. "We shouldn't be in here. Let's go." But Libby pulled away and went on down the hall. She didn't look back, but she could tell by the soft shuffle of footsteps that they were still behind her. As she opened the door at the end of the hall, they pressed in around her, and when she caught her breath in a sharp gasp, the others gasped too—a sharp, frightened, breathy chorus.

Someone was seated at the kitchen table. An enormous man with great, heavy shoulders was leaning forward across the table, his head resting on his outstretched arms. His blotched and bloated face was turned toward them, and for an awful minute Libby was sure that he was dead. But then she realized that the other sound she was hearing, a deep rasping noise, was the man's heavy, labored breathing. Her own lungs, which seemed to have stopped working, began again with a hungry gasp, but her mind and body were still frozen when Wendy pushed her aside and stepped around her.

"Hello, Mr. Greene," Wendy said. "Please excuse us for coming in this way and bothering you, but we rang the doorbell several times and no one . . ."

The man's eyes didn't open, and his heavy breathing continued. Wendy's voice was already dwindling away when Tierney interrupted her. "Forget it, Wendy. The dude is

179

locoed out. Smashed. Look." She pointed to the glass near the man's right hand and an empty bottle that lay on its side near his feet.

"Drunk?" Wendy whispered.

Tierney nodded. "Can't you smell it?" she said.

Libby noticed the smell then, too, a strong odor, sharp and at the same time sickly sweet. For a crazy moment something, perhaps the relief of knowing he wasn't dead or dying after all, made her want to laugh, but then she remembered.

"G.G.?" she said to Alex. "What about G.G.?"

Alex shook his head slowly and then suddenly nodded and almost ran from the room. Moving as fast as he could, Alex led the way down the hall and up the stairs to the second floor and then to a room at the back of the house.

It was obviously a boy's bedroom, cluttered and messy and decorated with pennants and pictures of sports stars. At first Libby thought the room was empty, but then someone gasped and pointed. G.G. was there all right, in the corner behind the bed, slumped forward against the wall like a limp rag doll. There was blood on the side of his face, and when they talked to him, he didn't answer.

19

That night, and then all through Thursday and Friday as well, Libby found it hard to concentrate. Even when she was busy with other things, talking to the family about entirely different matters, or sitting in class at school, parts of what had happened that afternoon kept flooding out again—and for brief moments, drowning out everything else. Whether the memories came in a slow, spreading trickle or a rushing tide, she would barely stop one leak when another would come oozing through.

At first, of course, it was only to be expected. In fact it had been necessary to remember everything in detail, for the police at first and then later, back at home, when she had gone over it all again for the family. And then at school on Friday after the whole story came out in the paper, people kept asking questions. But what Libby hadn't expected was how it would all keep coming back when she wasn't trying to remember—and didn't want to.

At one moment it might be just the interior of the house —the Greenes' Spanish hacienda—the look and feel of the dim hallway; the musty, cluttered rooms; and the deep, threatening silence. Or, more often, the sound of G.G.'s voice on the telephone, or a sudden visual image of him slumped against the wall in his room, or as he had looked later on the stretcher that carried him down the hall and out to the ambulance. Before bedtime on that Wednesday night some of those memories had already repeated themselves at least a hundred times, and Libby went to bed feeling tense and anxious and tired of remembering. Too tired, it seemed, even to write in her journal, although she tried.

Of course it had been fairly late at the time. After dinner the whole family sat in the library talking for a long time. They talked about G.G. and his father and what had happened that afternoon, and what might be going to happen next. Then for a while they had discussed alcoholism in general, and both Gillian and Cordelia told about people they had known who were alcoholics and what it sometimes did to their personalities, changing them from perfectly normal people to cruel and violent strangers. Three times during the evening Gillian called the hospital, and at last, on the third call, there was some news. G.G. was conscious and probably out of danger. Not long after that, Libby went to bed, but when she tried to write about what had happened, she was too tired. There was nothing too surprising about that, but it *was* surprising that she still wasn't able to the next day—and the next.

She didn't know why. She was still remembering it in bits and pieces all during the day, and sometimes at night in frightening nightmares, but when she sat down—sometimes in the Treehouse and sometimes in bed at night—and tried to write about it, she was unable to get past the first sentence. She supposed it was like writer's block, but she couldn't understand why it was happening now.

It was on Friday evening that she told Christopher about it. "I can't write about what happened to G.G.," she told him. "I don't know why. Mizzo says that it's very important to be able to write about feelings and that we should always try to write about things that we feel strongly about. But when I try to write about what happened that day, I get this tight, nervous feeling and my brain just starts spinning around and nothing comes out."

Christopher put down his newspaper, clear down on the coffee table instead of just on his lap, which meant that he was ready to talk for a long time if Libby wanted to. "Yes," he said. "It is very important to be able to write clearly and vividly about emotions. But there are times that feelings are too violent or too close to us to be put into words. When that's the case, one just has to wait."

"How long?" Libby asked. "How long do you think it will be before I can write about it?" She could hear the jittery tension in her voice, and Christopher must have heard it, too, because he reached out and pulled her into his lap and wrapped his arms around her. Cuddled down with her head against her father's chest, she felt herself relaxing.

"Not long," Christopher said in his soft, poetic voice. "Not long at all."

So Libby put the green notebook back in its hiding place in the Treehouse settee and went on trying to think about something else. But on Sunday morning she went up to her room right after breakfast and climbed out the window. In the Treehouse she got out the notebook and put it on the drum table. She even picked up her pen—and doodled some birds and flowers up and down the margins. But, at last, she shook her head and climbed on up to the triangular room and checked to see if the bird feeders needed filling before she went on up the ladder to the lookout.

It was a bright, clear spring morning. Looking out toward the river, she could see Christopher coming and going with the lawn mower, and Cordelia in her gardening dress and floppy sunhat, cutting irises and lilies. It was a familiar scene, the moving, sparkling river, the bright colors of flowers, and the widening, velvety swath of mowed lawn. She had seen it many times before, all of it—the lawn and flowers, and Christopher and Cordelia doing exactly the same kinds of things. But suddenly she was seeing it in a different way.

It was a mysterious feeling, deep and strong and comforting. A kind of steady, solid knowing that it was all there, around her and inside of her, and that all of it—the family and the house and the Treehouse, and everything she had ever learned or read or done—would always be there inside her, no matter what else happened. Christopher had mowed almost to the riverbank before Libby left the lookout room and went back down to the drum table and her journal.

It began with a phone call and G.G.'s voice calling—screaming—for help. And so we went there, the four of us, Alex and Tierney and Wendy and I. It was a large Spanish-style house, but inside it was dark and dirty, and in the kitchen we found his father lying across the kitchen table. He seemed to be asleep or maybe sick, but it turned out he was just extremely drunk. And then Alex remembered where

184

G.G.'s room was, and we went there and found him, only he was unconscious, and at first we thought he was dead.

She wrote the first page slowly and calmly, but after that her heart began to thud so hard it made her hands shake, and she wrote faster, with her handwriting getting more and more rough and scrawly.

He looked dead. I felt frozen, like nothing was working except my heart, which was pounding so hard and fast I could barely breathe. We were all frozen at first, I think, but then I put a blanket over G.G., and Wendy helped me. I didn't know whether to put the blanket over his head. He looked so dead, and I didn't want to look at him anymore and see his swollen face and the blood coming down out of his hair and across his forehead. But then, without either of us saying anything, we just didn't. I don't know why. We just didn't cover up his face, and I am glad we didn't, because he was alive after all, and somehow it seems that—if we'd covered up his head, it would have all been over, and he would have been dead. So Wendy and I covered him up all except his face, and then we stayed there with him while Alex and Tierney went to call the police.

She had to stop for a while then, until her hand stopped shaking, so it was several minutes before she went on.

Everyone is talking about it at school, and some of it has been in the paper. G.G.'s father was taken away to jail and then to a special hospital for alcoholics. There was an interview with him in last night's paper. He said, in the interview, that he was terribly sorry about what happened and that he plans to stay at the sanatorium until his alcohol problem is cured forever. I hope he means it.

Elliott thinks he means it and so does Gillian, but Cordelia doesn't. Cordelia says drunkards always say they're quitting, and she thinks Tony Greene ought to be put in prison for life. Gillian and Cordelia argued about it for quite a long time.

Libby had begun to write about Gillian and Cornelia's argument and how it related to what happened to G.G., but she'd only completed a line or two when she heard Gillian calling to say that Wendy was on the telephone—Wendy usually called several times a day on weekends. So Libby put the journal away, thinking she would have to find some time later on to finish writing about what had happened that terrible Wednesday afternoon.

But then there was a shopping trip with Gillian and Cordelia, and in the afternoon Tierney came over to play billiards, and it was quite late at night before she had a chance to write again. It was dark by then, so she only stayed in the Treehouse long enough to get the green notebook out of its hiding place in the settee. Back in her room she crawled into bed, opened Graham's safari writing desk, and got out a pen.

There was some unfinished business. What she fully intended to do was to continue writing about G.G., but then something caught her eye—Mercedes' latest letter, still lying where she had dropped it on her dresser. And suddenly, without even deciding to, she began to write something entirely different—the first letter she had written to Mercedes in a long, long time.

Dear Mercedes,
I'm sorry that it's been so long since I've written but . . .

She thought for perhaps as much as five or ten minutes before she went on.

. . . I've been angry at you because I blamed you for making me go to Morrison Middle School, and I HATED it. At least I did for a long time.

It turned out to be one of the longest letters Libby had ever written. She began by telling about how terrible Morrison Middle School had been at first and how she had lied to everyone so that she would be allowed to quit as soon as the school year was over. She told about the beginning of the writers' workshop and how frightened she had been about it, and how it had turned out to be so different from what she'd expected.

She also wrote about what happened to G.G., but only briefly, because she knew that Gillian and Christopher had already written to tell Mercedes all about it.

The last paragraph went . . .

So now the school year is almost over, and I really kind of want to go on going to Morrison next year. And I guess you would say that that's because your plan worked and I've been SOCIALIZED. Right? No! Wrong! I actually haven't made much progress at all at being socialized. I still get tense and jittery if I have to say anything in class, and I usually can't talk to people I don't know without being very nervous and making an idiot of myself. So I'm a long way from being really socialized. The only reason that I want to go on going to Morrison next year is that there are some people there that I like and some others that I am curious about and . . .

She stopped again and sat staring at what she had written. Staring and thinking and wondering—until her thoughts were interrupted by the sound of her cuckoo clock counting off the hours—it was eleven o'clock. And the next day was a school day.

So the letter ended right there, in mid-sentence.

. . . some people there that I like and some others that I am curious about and . . .
Wow! It's eleven o'clock.
Your SOCIALIZED *daughter,*
Libby

So she didn't get anything more written about G.G. that night, and the next day was a Monday with lots of extra homework. It was several days before she was able to write in the green notebook again, and when she finally did, she decided that that particular part of her journal—about the day they found G.G.—was as finished as it needed to be.

The FFW continued to meet. Only there were just the four of them now since Gary Greene was no longer a member or even a student at Morrison Middle School. The rumor was that after he'd been released from the hospital, he'd been sent to live with some relatives in another city.

But the reduced membership wasn't the only change. For one thing, there had been a definite decrease in what Mizzo would have called nonconstructive-type activity. They'd all noticed it—a whole different feeling at the workshop meetings. Everyone had commented on it from time to time, particularly Alex. And Alex himself was one of the things that had changed the most.

In the last few weeks, during what Alex called the "post-G.G. era," he seemed much less nervous and twitchy, and he did a lot more talking during the workshop sessions. As Tierney said, Alex Lockwood might not be very well coordinated in some ways, but there certainly wasn't anything wrong with his brain-mouth connection. Sometimes the rest of them complained about the amount of time Alex used up commenting and critiquing, as well as just running off at the mouth in general, but at the same time they all agreed that everything he had to say was interesting or funny, or both.

After a while they started calling him Alexander the Great—Libby started it actually—and pretty soon they were all doing it. "Here comes Alexander the Great," they would say, or "Alex the Great," and after a while just "The Great." And it was pretty obvious that "The Great" liked his new nickname, as well as all the extra attention he was getting.

In early May the workshop received a letter from Mizzo addressed to the FFW at 1177 Windward, and the return address was Morrison instead of San Francisco. Mizzo was out of the hospital but she wouldn't be coming back to school for two or three more weeks, so the time and place continued to be after school on Wednesdays at the McCall House. Usually they held the workshop in the Treehouse, but once, in cold, rainy weather, they met in the Great Hall in front of the fire. And always, after the workshop was over, there would be refreshments in the kitchen, and usually the family would be there too.

By now the workshop members and the family were well acquainted. Too well acquainted, Libby sometimes thought. In the kitchen after the workshop meeting it sometimes seemed that Gillian and Cordelia, and now and then Elliott, were doing most of the talking, telling old "famous people I have known" or "exotic places I have traveled" stories. Stories that Libby had heard dozens of times but that Tierney and Wendy and Alex, for some reason, seemed to find fascinating.

190

Gillian was perhaps the biggest favorite. Tierney and Wendy loved to get her talking about her life in Paris. And Alex had discovered about Gillian and Cordelia and politics, and he liked to bring up political subjects and then just sit back, grinning, and enjoy the fireworks. Subjects like Franklin Delano Roosevelt. Libby tried to tell him that mentioning subjects like FDR in front of Gillian and Cordelia was just asking for trouble, but he just smiled fiendishly and said, "Yeah, I know. Exciting, isn't it?"

Sometimes Libby actually got a little frustrated—like when she had something important to say and no one was listening. It was rather ironical really—the fact that she'd worried so much about what the FFW would think of the family and now she sometimes wished they liked each other a little less.

The workshop itself was coming along fine. Alex had started a new parody, on detective stories this time, and Tierney had given him permission to use some ideas from the one that she had written. Ideas like calling his detective Hatchet, instead of Spade or Hammer.

Wendy's latest story, the one set in the twenties, was getting more interesting as it went along, particularly after the heroine's rich father lost all his money in the market crash and she started having to sell all her beautiful clothing to buy food. Tierney's critique was that Wendy should always have her characters go broke, because her stories were much faster paced when she didn't have to describe what everyone was wearing every couple of paragraphs. To Libby's surprise, Wendy seemed to take the remark as a compliment—but maybe that was because of the way Tierney said

191

it. Tierney—well, everybody really—was getting a little better at constructive criticism.

After they more or less finished the "Island Adventure" collaboration, they mailed it to Mizzo. And a few days later she mailed it back with her critique of what they had written. Of course Libby read it as soon as the letter arrived, but she decided not to tell the others and surprise them with it at the next workshop meeting.

So, on the next Wednesday, Libby was planning to start the meeting by reading Mizzo's letter. It was a nice, warm day, and they were meeting as usual in the Treehouse. As soon as they were all seated and Wendy had marked everyone present in the roll book, Libby told them about Mizzo's critique.

"Hey, great!" Alex said. "I'll bet she really liked the part where the movie company shows up on the island and we all get jobs as extras."

"Sure she did," Tierney said sarcastically, who had never thought much of Alex's movie-company idea. "Particularly the part where we don't explain how come the movie guys go away in all their fancy boats and leave us still marooned on the island."

So Alex said that was Hollywood for you, and Tierney said what did he know about Hollywood, and Libby finally had to bang on the table and yell to get them to shut up and let her start reading Mizzo's letter.

She had just read, "It's a riot. I laughed until my broken ribs ached"—as usual, Mizzo started out constructively by mentioning what she liked best—when suddenly Wendy said, "Hey, listen. Somebody's coming."

As soon as Libby stopped reading, they all could hear it,

192

the rusty squeak of the iron staircase as someone climbed up toward the Treehouse.

"Gillian, maybe?" Wendy asked, but Libby shook her head. None of the family ever came up to the Treehouse.

The creaking noise went around the trunk, getting closer and closer, and then someone was on the landing, pushing the door open—and then standing there in the doorway. It was G.G.

It was hard to believe. After seeing him over and over again in imagination the way he had looked that last day, on the floor of his room, it was hard to believe that he was actually standing there looking just like his normal self. His wide, blunt-looking face was just the way it had always been, and even his halfway threatening smile seemed unchanged. And as they all sat there staring, speechless with surprise, the smile widened.

"Hey, you lucky people," he said. "Look who's back."

"Wha—wha—wha?" Alex was beginning to stutter, when Wendy pulled herself together and interrupted.

"Well, *HI!*, G.G.," she said, with her best TV-hostess smile. "Where did you come from?"

"Yeah," Tierney said. "I thought you were living up in Chico now."

G.G. took off his backpack and sat down. "I'm back," he said. He took out his notebook and kept his eyes on it as he went on. "I'm back with my dad. He got out of the clinic last week, and I came back to live with him. He's—he's all right now. He hasn't had a drink in six weeks. Besides, it was no big deal. I just had this little concussion from hitting my head on something when I fell down. Well, yeah, he knocked me down. See, he told me not to use the phone because he thought I was going to call the police or my mom or something, so when he caught me calling you guys, he blew his top. But we're getting along great now. So, hey. Let's get started. Who's reading?"

So they went on with the meeting. For the first few minutes G.G. was quieter and more polite than usual, but before the workshop was over, he was pretty much back to normal—making sarcastic comments and laughing harder at things that were embarrassing than things that were funny. And when Libby asked him if he wanted to read, he said he didn't have anything ready but he was working on another war story and he'd have it ready to read next time.

Next time. The thought gave Libby a sinking feeling and, looking around at the others, she could tell that they were feeling pretty much the same way. None of them said anything, but it was easy to tell what they were thinking.

G.G. left early. "I'm outta here," he said, getting up suddenly and putting on his backpack. "I got to get home a little early because my dad and I are going out to dinner. See ya." Then he went out and down the stairs, leaving the door open.

Tierney got up, closed the door, leaned against it, and groaned. "Okay, you dudes. You been breaking the Ten Commandments, or what?"

Wendy looked shocked. "What do you mean?"

"I mean somebody must have done something really evil to deserve this."

Alex's face was twitching, and he looked really angry. "It's no joke, Laurent," he told Tierney. "We have to do something to get rid of him. It's been so—so great without him. So now we have to go back to old Gary the Ghoul

194

throwing his weight around and entertaining himself by tormenting everybody. I think what we ought to do is vote him out of the workshop. Oh, I know it won't stick while we're still meeting here, unless somebody wants to take up karate. But once Mizzo is back and we start meeting at school again, we can tell her we've voted him out and I'll bet she'll go along with it. You know how big she is on democracy."

"Yeah," Tierney said, nodding thoughtfully.

But Wendy looked worried. "I don't know. I kind of hate to do that. Don't you think that maybe if we let him stay in, he'll kind of change? Like, it seemed to me he's changed a little bit already. You know, like today I noticed that sometimes when he was doing that look, you know, the way he does . . ." Wendy pulled her eyebrows together and curled up one side of her mouth, which made everyone laugh because there was no way Wendy was going to look anything like G.G. "I know," she went on, smiling ruefully. "But like, I was just noticing today that when he did that— it looks mean, all right, but underneath it's more like . . ." She stopped and frowned thoughtfully. "Scared?" she asked.

Libby nodded hard. "Yes," she said. "Scared. I thought so too. That's really funny, because I thought that same thing a long time ago."

No one said anything else for quite a while. Finally Tierney said, "What do you think? You think his dad is really going to stay off the sauce?"

Alex shrugged. "Who knows. Mostly they don't, I guess. G.G. was talking like he believed it, but I'll bet . . ."

There was another long pause. Libby was thinking about the story G.G. wrote called "Eric." About the boy who waited and waited for something terrible, not ever knowing when it was going to happen or how bad it would be. "Remember that story he wrote . . . ?" she started to say, but then she stopped because the way the others were nodding, she could tell they were already remembering.

"Well," Wendy said, "what I want to say is—I mean, like, I know it wouldn't be easy but . . ." She got that far before Tierney slapped her on the back so hard that what she was going to say turned into a startled gasp.

"So what?" Tierney said. "EASY is not necessarily where it's at. Right?"

Libby was the first to repeat it, and Wendy was next, as soon as she got her breath back. Alex was the last, and he groaned a little first, but finally even he managed it.

"Right!" Alex said, with a sigh. "So it's unanimous. Don't ask me why, but it is. Looks like our next collaboration is going to be 'The Return of G.G.' Do you think we can write it?"

Libby thought maybe they could.

ABOUT THE AUTHOR

ZILPHA KEATLEY SNYDER has written many distinguished books for children, including *The Egypt Game, The Headless Cupid,* and *The Witches of Worm,* all Newbery Honor books and American Library Association Notable Books for Children.

Libby on Wednesday was suggested, she says, by "having had the opportunity to appear as a speaker at many individual schools as well as at districtwide Young Authors' Festivals. At such times I have met many young people who, at the age of nine through the early teens, are already dedicated, industrious, and obviously talented writers—writers who discuss with the passion of the deeply involved such things as genre, style, point of view, as well as that dreaded curse, writer's block. All the characters in *Libby on Wednesday* were inspired by certain young writers I have met at such events."

Zilpha Keatley Snyder lives in Marin County, California.